Unwrapping You
Written by De' Andrea

Disclaimer

'Tis the season for healing and rekindling

Please note that while this story takes place

during the holiday season, it touches on the

subject of violent crimes and the aftermath.

Chapter 1

I knew exactly what it was the minute Calvin entered the room with that phone up to his ear. His eyes quickly darted in my direction.

"Yeah, I'll be there in fifteen to twenty minutes."

Disappointed yet again, I slipped off my heels.

"Aaliyah..." He sighed after hanging up.

"Just save it and go on about your business."

He came over to where I sat on our king sized bed and caressed my thick thigh. "I'll make it up to you."

I forcefully shoved his hand off me. "Tonight was supposed to make up for all of the times before this one!"

"I know, but the hospital is short staffed. Cut me some slack, baby."

I let my silence express my feelings as I grabbed my cell phone, rose from the bed, and stormed out of the room.

I descended the spiral staircase while unzipping my mini dress, only pausing to step out of it. Trudging into the kitchen, I grabbed a bottle of Stella Rose moscato and carried it into the living room. After popping the bottle, I sat back on the forest green velvet sofa. Calvin ambled into the room.

"Liyah, baby, don't be mad. I'll make it up to you. I promise." He reached into his pants pocket and retrieved his bank card. "Here. Take my card and do some online shopping, no budget."

When I didn't move to reach for it, he placed it on the glass tabletop. "Liyah, I know you're not starting that childish silent treatment."

"What's the point of me repeating the same shit over and over if you act like those big ass ears and that brain inside your jughead is malfunctioning?! Bye, Cal!" I waved my hand dismissively. "I'll see you when I see you!"

"Bye, Liyah. I love you. I'll see you sometime tomorrow." He stood there waiting for a response.

"Mhmm..."

Exhaling loudly, he turned and slithered out the front door.

I had a mind to call my friend girl, Apryl, and give her a good tongue lashing since she was the one that set us up. *"He's fine, single, no kids, and he's a doctor!"* she'd said. *"He's older than you, which I think is perfect."* Having nothing to lose, I'd agreed to go on the blind date. The brother was tall, handsome with a full beard, perfect teeth, butterscotch skin tone, and he was very refined. Nothing I'd experienced, so I was intrigued. The date went great, and things took off like a rocket. Calvin wooed me. He had no problem fitting me into his busy schedule. Almost every free moment that he had was spent with me, and the sex... The sex was amazing and frequent. You would've thought that Janet Jackson's "Any Time, Any Place" was inspired by us. Within the first year of our relationship, he popped the question and moved me into his house.

These days, we were in a completely different space. Calvin was now just the man whose home I resided in. Everything was lacking. Sex was nonexistent, and I couldn't recall the last time we'd gone on a date or even relaxed at home together.

The ping of my phone alerted me of an email, pulling me away from my thoughts of my relationship woes. I clicked on the notification that redirected me to the Gmail app. Clicking on the email, I read the message from my publisher telling me that if I didn't put out a page turner by the end of January then my ass was grass. Not long ago, I was a force to be reckoned with in the literary industry, penning numerous chart topping urban fiction and erotica novels along with a book of poetry. Now my writing career, like the rest of my life, was in shambles. I hadn't produced anything in almost seven months. The readers had been on my ass so bad that I'd deactivated all of my social media accounts. Deciding that I should attempt to write, I scooped up my laptop and headed out the side door to the pool area.

The water from the infinity pool illuminated a light blue hue as the city lights below the hills shone brightly, making it what some would deem the perfect ambiance. I maneuvered my bare bottom around the cushioned lounge chair until I was comfortable and opened my laptop. Unsure of what to type, I read the ten thousand words that I'd already written aloud to see how it flowed. After reading the last paragraph, I was still stuck on stupid. It wasn't that I didn't want to write. The inspiration was lacking, especially since my last two books were loosely based on the happy times of my relationship. I closed my laptop, contemplating starting a new work about a bad bitch in a stale relationship with a renowned doctor.

"Hrs & Hrs" by Muni Long blared from my phone's speaker, indicating that Calvin was calling.

"How ironic. I can barely get twenty minutes," I mumbled before answering. "Hello?"

"Hey, babe! What you doing?" Calvin greeted, like he hadn't pissed me off less than an hour ago.

"Hey..." I sighed. "Was attempting to write, but I got nothing."

I noticed that there was absolutely no noise in his background. Was he really at work?

"Cal, where are you? Are you cheating on me?" I blurted.

I glanced down at my bare breasts and wide hips. Was he no longer attracted to me? That would explain why he'd lost interest in our relationship.

"Liyah, no! I would never! I'm at the hospital in the break room brewing a cup of joe to keep me going through the night. What's wrong with you?!" he asked with an attitude.

"We're fading."

"Fading? What is that supposed to mean? You're talking crazy. Are you drunk?"

"No, I'm not drunk. Just... nevermind."

"Well, I was calling because I have some good news."

I perked up a little. "What's that?"

"Doctor Schumichael agreed to work a double shift tomorrow, so I'll get to spend the day with you," he said enthusiastically. "I was thinking we could have lunch and do a little shopping. Then you can be my second helping of dessert when we make it home."

"I like the sound of that," I grinned.

"Paging Dr. Mathers!" A nurse's voice called over the intercom.

"Shit! I didn't even get to drink my coffee," he griped. "I gotta go. I love you, Liyah."

"Love you too," I remarked before ending the call.

Maybe all the hoping, wishing, and praying that I'd been doing for us was finally paying off.

***

I felt an overwhelming sense of homesickness as I prepared for bed. This was the third night in a row. I missed my mama, the smell of her house, her cooking. I missed my crazy little sister, EJ. I talked to them everyday, but I suddenly needed to physically be in their presence. I didn't know where this was coming from because I'd been in California for almost three years now. I'd experienced so much pain in my home state that I'd moved and never looked back, even though my former therapist had said I was strong enough to at least visit. I reached over to the nightstand and grabbed the bottle of melatonin, needing something to knock me out. I swallowed the pills, flicked off the lamp, and turned onto my side as a tear escaped.

***

The following day, I gathered my hair into a messy bun and kept my look cute and casual by going with a sleeveless heather gray midi dress and gray Chucks. I tossed my Marc Jacobs tote over my shoulder and headed downstairs to where Calvin waited.

"I'm ready!" I announced as he turned around with lust filled eyes.

"Come here." He licked his full lips while beckoning me over to the couch.

The anticipation of finally getting what I yearned for had me wet. As I made my way over, he instructed me to bend over the back of the couch. After doing as I was told, he raised my dress above my rounded hips and dove head first into my goodies, licking and slurping as if his life depended on it.

"Wait..." My legs quivered and almost gave out.

If I wasn't anchored between him and the couch, I would've slid to the tile floors. He rose to his feet with my juices and cream decorating his full beard. Grasping my neck and tilting my head upward, he stuck his tongue down my throat while slipping inside my honey pot.

"Damn, baby..." he grunted as he proceeded to beat my kitty.

Unable to formulate any words, I whimpered, moaned, and groaned. Sweat beaded around my curly baby hairs as my climax neared.

Still on cloud nine, I reclined my seat a tad bit as soft jazz floated from the G-wagon's speakers. I yawned loudly and drifted off to sleep.

"Hey, son!" The sound of Calvin's mother's voice awakened me.

"Hey, ma!" he beamed.

"Hey, Ms. Katherine!" I spoke while glaring at him as he helped her climb into the backseat. "I didn't know you'd be joining us."

"I thought, since we were going shopping, she may as well tag along and pick out something to wear to the hospital's winter gala."

"And I thought this would be a chance for us to have some one on one time, but I should've known better. It's always some bullshit with you."

And the gala is in three days. Why is she just now searching for a dress? I wondered.

"Watch your language!" he scolded.

"Watch your actions!" I retorted.

"Let's not do this in front of mama."

"I think maybe I should just go back inside. I'll see you guys another time," Ms. Katherine commented.

"No, mama. I want you to come." He closed the passenger door.

I should've known something was up by the way that he'd handled me before we left. I guess good dick was supposed to pacify me as he slid his mother in the mix. Don't get things misconstrued. His mother was a sweet lady, and I liked her. It's just that this wasn't what I had in mind.

"I'm sorry, Ms. Katherine," I apologized.

"It's ok, baby."

Calvin slid back into the driver's seat with his lips pressed into a tight line. The tension was so thick that you could cut it with a knife. Ms. Katherine cleared her throat.

"So, Choc, when is your next release?" she queried, calling me by my family given nickname, which was also my pen name. "I'm ready to get lost in another one of your books."

I let out a frustrated breath. "Hopefully at the beginning of next year. I've been going through some changes, so it's been difficult to write."

"Well, whenever you do, I'm sure it'll be something great." She reached up and patted my left shoulder. "CJ, I'm so excited about the winter gala! I hope you win doctor of the year!"

"He practically lives there, so he should," I muttered.

He cut his eyes at me. "I hope so too, mama."

***

"Sweetie, are you okay?" Ms. Katherine eyed me with concern as I nibbled on my sushi.

I plastered on a fake smile. "Yes, ma'am."

"I'll be right back." Calvin excused himself from the table and headed to the nearest restroom.

"Ms. Katherine, I want to apologize to you again," I began. "I shouldn't have acted that way in front of you."

"It's ok, sweetie. I know that your issue is with my son, not me." She reached across the table to grasp my free hand. "You wanna talk about it?"

"I know that Calvin's dad was also a doctor. Did he spend most of his time working?"

"Yes, Calvin Sr. was gone most of the time."

"And that didn't bother you?"

She chuckled. "It did at first, but I guess I got used to it. Plus we had CJ very early in our relationship. The financial well being of myself and my child became my only priority, so I stuck it out."

"Ms. Katherine, I love your son, but these days it seems like he loves his job more than he does me. And no offense, but I don't want to end up like you. I've tried my best to voice my issues, but it always falls on deaf ears."

"I see, and none taken. Baby, let me tell you something." She let go of my hand and reached for her beverage. After taking a sip, she continued, "If he isn't listening, you have to show him."

"Yes, ma'am."

Calvin returned to our table. "What are you ladies talking about?"

"Nothing," his mom replied while winking at me.

"You like this?" Ms. Katherine held up a beautiful beaded gown.

"Yes, ma'am." I nodded.

"I think I'm gonna go try this one on." She walked off in search of an employee.

I pulled a satin rose gold pants set from one of the racks. This was something that I thought my mama would like. Just to be sure, I FaceTimed her.

"Hot girl, Rozlyn!" I grinned into the camera when she picked up.

"What's up witchu, Choc?" She giggled.

"I'm at this boutique with my mother-in-law, and I see this badass suit that you might like. See?" I flipped the camera and held it up.

"Girl, yesss!" she squealed. "Too bad I can't receive it today. It would be perfect for the Christmas trip that me and my man are taking."

"What man?" I gasped.

"His name is Andrew." She laughed.

"You really going somewhere, or are you just saying something?"

"I'm really going on a trip with my boo."

"Aww man! So when I come down for the holidays, you won't be there." I pouted.

"You haven't been home for anything in years, but you wanna wait until I plan to go out of town to finally come."

"I really miss ya'll, and lately I've been feeling unbalanced." I blew out.

"We miss you too, and I know what you mean, baby. That's exactly why I'm leaving for a few days, but I'll be back the day after Christmas. EJ will be here though."

"Roz!" a deep voice hollered in the background.

"I gotta go, baby."

"Alright, but ma, don't tell EJ that I'm coming. I wanna surprise her."

"I won't. I love you, Choc."

"I love you too. I'll see you soon." I blew a kiss before hanging up.

With Ms. Katherine's words replaying in my mind, I didn't know when or if I wanted to tell Calvin about my plans. I was on the fence about whether I should continue to try to make whatever this was between us work.

***

"Liyah, the way you acted in front of my mother today is unacceptable," Calvin stated sternly the minute we made it back home.

"I know that, and I apologized to her again when you went to the restroom. I was under the impression that it was gonna be just us."

"I should have told you. I'm sorry." He grabbed me and kissed the top of my head. "And it is just us for the rest of the night."

***

"Cal, we have to start spending more time together. I don't care if we just sit in the house. I just want to be close to you," I stated as we soaked in the tub. "You have to start back making our relationship a priority if you want us to last."

"Ok, baby."

"You're saying ok, but are you really understanding me this time?" I leaned forward and pivoted to look into his eyes.

"Yes, Aaliyah." He kissed my lips and stuck his hand underneath the water to rub between my folds.

My hips wound involuntarily as he slipped a digit inside.

Needing more than a finger, I broke the kiss. "Let's get out."

The only thing we dried were our feet before he scooped me up. Ankles locked around his waist, I suckled his tongue as he carried me over to our bed. He laid me down gently, lowered his frame over mine, and slid inside my slippery walls.

"I love you," he whispered.

"I love you too." Grabbing the sides of his face, I brought his lips back to mine.

Chapter 2

"You look beautiful, baby," Calvin whispered in my ear and planted a tender kiss on the side of my neck.

"Thank you." I smiled before tilting my head upward and puckering my lips for a kiss.

The hospital had gone all out for their first annual winter gala. They'd rolled out the red carpet in front of the building's entrance where the who's who of the medical field posed for photographers representing various health publications. I flashed a Colgate worthy smile as I stood beside my man. After being shuffled along, we finally made it inside the venue and to our reserved table a few feet from the stage setup. The black and gold decorations were nothing short of beautiful.

"This is nice," I commented.

Once everyone was seated, the event got underway. A petite blonde approached the podium that was set up. "Good evening! I'm Nancy Wright, one of the UCLA Medical Center's board of directors. As you all know, tonight is a celebration of our devoted medical staff and all of those who pour so much of themselves into our healthcare system. I know you're ready to eat, drink, and party, but we'd like to honor some of our key people while we're all sober."

She paused to share a chuckle with the audience before continuing, "These awards that we're about to present were voted on by the entire hospital staff, so if you receive one, please know that your peers think very highly of you."

She went on to present awards to various people from different departments, eventually making it to the category that everyone in the room seemed to be anticipating. Men and women, whom I'm assuming were doctors, twitched nervously as Nancy pulled out a black envelope.

"And now for the moment most of you have been waiting for... The award for doctor of the year goes to..." She peeled the envelope open and her eyes enlarged. "Dr. Calvin Mathers!"

The room erupted with applause.

"My baby!" Ms. Katherine leaned over and squeezed him.

When she let him go, he softly kissed my cheek before heading to the podium.

"Congratulations, Dr. Mathers! You certainly deserve it!" Nancy beamed. "Give us a few words."

"I don't do what I do for accolades, but I certainly accept this award. Thank you to my peers for taking notice of my dedication. I truly love what I do, and the hospital and my patients will always be my top priority. Again, thank you!" He raised his plaque before stepping down and making his way back towards our table.

Tears clouded my vision as I stared down at the black table cloth. Here I was supporting and trying to love a man who wouldn't meet me halfway to even try to make this work. He'd confirmed it in front of a room full of people. I'd always come last, so there was no hope for us. He'd lied to me.

"I'm going to find the restroom," I mumbled, unsure if Ms. Katherine heard me or not.

***

Luckily, the restroom was empty, and it was one of those that was made for one occupant at a time. Tears rained down my chocolate face as I locked the door behind me.

I didn't realize how long I'd been standing there until there was a knock, and then the sound of Ms. Katherine's voice came from the other side of the door.

"Baby, are you alright? You've been in there for a while."

"Yes, ma'am. I'm fine," I fibbed. "I'll be out in a minute."

"Aaliyah, sweetie, open the door."

She stepped inside and clutched my face. "Aww, baby..."

"He said one thing to me, and then he got up there saying something completely different!" I cried. "The hospital will always be his top priority! Do you know how stupid I feel?! I'm sitting up here wearing his ring while he's basically saying fuck my feelings!"

"I understand, baby, but listen to me. You fix your face, and go back out there with CJ. This is obviously what he wanted, so let him have his moment. Tomorrow is yours. You can do whatever you so choose then. Do you understand what I'm saying?" She used her fingertips to wipe away my tears.

I nodded.

"Good. Now let's fix your face. Do you have makeup in your clutch?"

"No, ma'am."

"Lucky for you, I keep foundation, a brush, mascara, and a lippie in my pocketbook. And we're about the same complexion. Come on." She led me towards the mirror.

***

"Are you okay?" Calvin asked as we made it back to the table.

"Yeah. My sister, she called me needing to vent." I leaned over and kissed his cheek. "Congratulations on your award."

"Thanks." He grinned proudly.

I grabbed my fork and began eating the food that was waiting for me. Keeping my eyes trained on the white and gold china, I chewed and swallowed the bland Filet mignon.

Cal eyed me skeptically. "You sure you're okay?"

"Yes."

Nancy moseyed her way over to where we sat. "Congratulations again, Calvin!"

She gave him a pat on the back before directing her attention to Ms. Katherine. "It's good to see you again, Ms. Mathers."

Then she trained her baby blue eyes on me. "And who might this beautiful young woman be?"

"This is my fiancée, Aaliyah," Calvin replied.

"It's nice to meet you, Aaliyah. You should be extremely proud of Calvin. Our hospital is lucky to have him."

I plastered on a Chesire cat grin. "It's nice to meet you as well. And I'm extremely proud of him."

***

A tipsy Calvin planted wet kisses on my neck. Irritated, I stepped away from him, but he just didn't seem to get the hint as he gripped one of my buttcheeks.

"I'm not in the mood, Cal," I stated while raking his hand off me.

"Come on, Liyah...I wanna make love to you." He pressed his body against mine, his erect penis poking me in the lower back.

"Where's your plaque?"

"It's on the dresser. Why?"

"Go get it and rub your dick up and down it until you cum, or better yet go find a crack in the hospital walls and stick it in there since that's your top priority."

"Excuse me?!"

I tugged my nightshirt over my head. "You heard me."

"You know, you've been being a bitch just about the entire night! What is your problem?"

Ignoring him, I climbed into bed.

"It's like you're hellbent on ruining my night! Are you jealous because I have something going for myself and you don't?!" he spat.

"Muthafucka, I know you didn't!" I cackled as his face twisted. "I hate to break it to you, but you ain't all that! Look at you! Yes, you have all these awards and certificates, but outside of that, you don't have much of an identity. Who are you without that title? You're almost forty years old, but working day in and day out is making you look closer to fifty. You don't have a family, nobody to carry on your legacy, nobody to leave all this useless materialistic shit to." I gestured around the room. "You haven't acquired the things that really matter, so in reality, you, sir, don't have shit going for yourself. Good night."

His jaws were still on the floor as I wiggled around and made myself comfortable underneath the sheets. A few moments later, he snatched the top comforter from the bed along with his pillow.

Good! Now I can book a flight. I thought.

As he exited, I got up to shut the door behind him.

After scouring the net, I found a flight to New Orleans for 11 a.m. I set an alarm, deciding that it would be best to get up at about eight so I'd have time to pack my belongings.

***

Calvin was nowhere to be found when I awakened the next morning. He either didn't care or assumed I would be there whenever he made it back home. I filled my favorite mug with southern pecan flavored coffee and cautiously carried it upstairs.

After taking a sip and scalding my tongue, I placed the mug down on the nightstand and headed towards the his and hers walk-in closet.

"What should I take?"

My eyes scanned the numerous racks and shelves. Choosing to go with the basics, a couple of favorites, and a few of my designer handbags, I pulled out three suitcases and a carry on. When I was sure that I'd gotten all I wanted, I zipped everything up and slipped on an oversized sweatsuit. Now I had one last decision to make. Did I want to just go ghost or leave Cal a note?

"If I leave a note, what can I say?" I flopped down on the edge of the bed and took another sip of the now lukewarm coffee. "Dear Calvin, fuck ya?"

I chortled at the notion. Opening the top drawer of the nightstand, I grabbed the notepad and pen that I always kept there.

Dear Calvin, After jotting down the greeting, I tore away that sheet and balled it up. This was a good riddance, peace out note, not a love letter. I started over.

Cal,

I've come to realize that we're on two different pages when it comes to this relationship and that you

cannot love me the way that I need you to. So this is goodbye.

I placed the notepad on the nightstand beside the mug and exhaled loudly while sitting my engagement ring in the center of it. After checking my left wrist for the time, I got up to lug my bags downstairs and wait for my Uber.

***

As I sat in one of the plastic seats waiting to board my flight, I pulled out my phone to call my mother.

"Hey, ma! What you doing?" I smiled the second the call connected.

"On the road to North Cackalacky. He decided to get me out of here before you know..." She cleared her throat. "What you doing?"

"I'm actually at the airport getting ready to head that way."

"Oh, you're early. When you said you were coming, I thought you meant a day or two before Christmas, not a whole week and a half."

"Welp, I changed my plans."

"Is your fiancé coming with you?" she asked.

"No, ma'am. It's just me, and I plan to stay a while," I stated.

"Good. I really missed you, baby, and I'm glad you're finally strong enough to come back."

"Me too."

When it came to inner strength and the emotions that my return would trigger, I was very unsure.

The announcement of my flight sounded through the airport.

"They just called my flight. I'll shoot you a text when I land."

"Ok, sweetie. I love you."

"I love you too," I responded before ending the call.

Chapter 3

As I pushed the pedal of my rental across The Causeway, I adjusted the stereo's volume a little bit higher and bobbed my head to Boosie's "Set It Off". Being back on Louisiana soil was a different feeling all in itself. Unable to contain my excitement about being back, I decided to go ahead and call my sister. The phone rang and went to voicemail, but a few seconds later, she texted me letting me know that she was at work.

Pressing the microphone icon, I spoke, "Well, that's too damn bad because I'm headed to your hood!"

My phone's flash illuminated inside the car as her name popped up on the screen.

"Choc, quit playing!" she whispered harshly.

"EJ, I'm not playing. I'm a little less than an hour away."

"Oh my God!" she squealed. "I'm about to cry!"

"What time do you get off?"

"Supposed to be five o'clock, but let me know when you make it into town. I'mma fake sick."

"Alright." I giggled. "I think I'm gonna stop and get some rice and wings. You want some?"

"Hell yeah!" she responded. "I gotta go, but text me the second you make it here."

Calvin called the minute she hung up.

"Hello?" I answered dryly.

"Hey, Liyah. What are you doing?" he asked.

"I'm out and about tending to some business."

"I was calling to let you know that I'm gonna be a few hours late getting home."

"Okay. That's fine," I said calmly.

"Oh..." Surprise laced his voice. "Well, alright. I love you."

"Mhmm..." I hit the red X icon, ending the call.

***

I reduced my speed as I rounded the curve in the main road leading into my small hometown. One of the best food spots ever was a few yards away, and my mouth watered at the thought of what I was about to devour.

As I parked close to the convenience store doors, I read the new signs that were displayed behind the glass windows.

Making sure to grab my cell phone and tuck it into my handbag, I exited the car and headed towards the heavy glass door. The smell of seafood and other fried artery clogging foods hit my nostrils. My stomach talked loudly as I turned left by the cooler area where I stopped to pick up two bottles of Big Shot sodas, or as we called them down here, cold dranks. I made a loop around the rear of the small store and waited in line behind the other customers that were waiting to place orders.

"Anybody getting seafood?" one of the servers walked down and asked.

"Actually, I am." I read the price list. "Let me get six pounds of crawfish, but will you separate it into two three pound bags?"

"Sure." She smiled politely.

As the line moved towards the right of the store, I stepped up to the food display.

"Hi!" I grinned at the girl taking orders in the deli area. "How are you today?"

"I'm doing fine. What can I get for you?" she asked.

"Let me get two wing plates," I replied. "And that'll be it. I like your braids by the way."

"Thank you!" she remarked while hurriedly dishing up and bagging my food.

Satisfied that I may have brightened someone's day, I got in line at the register. I had a soft spot for people working at places like this because some folks could be so rude and cutthroat for no reason, straight assholes.

"What's up, Mr. Chang!" I greeted the store's owner.

His round face lit up with a smile so wide that his slanted eyes were no longer visible. "Choc! Is that you?! Long time!"

"I know! How have you been?"

"Very, very good!"

"Choc?!" the girl behind the counter exclaimed. "As in the writer?!"

I nodded. "Yes, ma'am! That's me!"

"Wow! I love your books! I've read them all on my Kindle."

"Aww thank you!" My face warmed. "What's your name?"

"Shanice."

"Well, Shanice, I'll order you some paperbacks and sign them for you."

"Ooh Wee! Thank you so much!" she squealed.

"Can I get some goddamn service please?!" this big beer gut man hollered.

I rolled my eyes at his rudeness before directing my attention back to Mr. Chang.

"I have those bags of crawfish, two plates, and these." I placed the drinks on the counter as he totaled everything up, excluding them.

After paying, I scooped up the large cardboard box that contained everything.

"It was good seeing you, Choc," Mr. Chang remarked.

"It was good seeing you too, but I'll be back real soon. May I have some extra plastic bags?"

He stuffed some into the box, and I headed to the exit.

"Thank you." I smiled at the young boy who held the door open for me.

I spread the plastic bags across the passenger seat and sat the box on top to prevent seafood juice from leaking onto the upholstery. Before backing out of the parking spot, I shot EJ a text.

Navigating the car down the side entrance of the parking lot, I decided to spend the block just to take in my old stomping grounds. The veterinarian's office, the only one in town, was still up and running and so was the funeral home a few yards away. I put on my turn signal and cruised down the road that led to my old high school. A sense of nostalgia washed over me as I peered over at the emblem decorating the school's sign. I recalled the time when I'd been one of the most despised and wanted girls in the building. But I only had eyes for my brother's best friend, who was three years older, and he treated me like a little sister until the summer after I graduated. It was on like a pot of neck bones then! I chuckled at the memories. Driving around the school and through the back gate, I headed in the direction of my childhood home.

I pulled into the driveway of my mother's hunter green and ivory painted house and awaited EJ's arrival. A few minutes later, she pulled up and hopped out of her Toyota Camry.

"Choc!" She just about squeezed the life out of me.

"EJ!" I choked out.

Her sniffles indicated her tears of joy.

"EJ, don't cry! You gon' get me started." I pulled back and wiped her round face.

My baby sister, Eleisha Jhanel, was the spitting image of our mama. They were the same short stature, same brickhouse build, and even shared the exact same beauty mark on the left side of their face right below their full bottom lip. Their only difference was their complexions. EJ was the color of toffee while mama was a redbone.

"Damn, big sis!" She looked me up and down before twirling me around. "You done got thick!"

I had put on a good amount of weight, but depression will do that to you. Thankfully, mine went to all the right places.

"Girl..." I waved her off and headed to the passenger side to get our food.

"Ooh, what you got?" EJ stood on her toes trying to peek inside the box.

"Just some hot wing plates, crawfish, and cold dranks," I replied.

"And I haven't eaten all day either! I'm about to tear this food up!"

I followed her up the five steps and onto the porch.

"Let's wash our hands and eat out here," she suggested. "The breeze feels nice."

I placed the box down on the wooden floor of the wraparound porch as she unlocked the door.

The smell of apple cinnamon invaded my nose. I stopped for a second and gazed around the living room. There was a Christmas tree in one corner, with lots of presents underneath, the majority being the ones that I'd sent. My eyes swept over the numerous framed photos of EJ, my late brother Brandon, and I.

"Girl, come on here! I'm starving!" EJ pulled me along to the kitchen.

"It feels weird being here again. How do you look at those pictures everyday without getting sad?" I asked as I lathered up my hands underneath the warm water.

She tore off a paper towel. "I do get sad sometimes, but I'm used to seeing them. How do you go without having pictures of him? You don't have days where you just want to see him?"

"Yes, but I fall back on what's stored here and here." I pointed to my head and my chest.

She quietly removed the roll of paper towels from the holder and tucked it underneath her arm before leading me out of the kitchen and back outside.

"Decisions, decisions," I mumbled as I debated whether to eat the seafood or the wing plate. There was no way my stomach could hold both.

Going with the plate, I opened up the styrofoam box to drown my shrimp fried rice in duck sauce when a black Dodge Challenger with tinted windows and bass beating pulled into the driveway of the house across the street.

"Aye, check this out!" EJ nudged me with her elbow.

The driver's side door opened, and one black and white Nike Dunk met the pavement as whoever it was extended their long leg. My curiosity about who this was that had her all worked up grew larger than my appetite. He stepped out, and my mouth dropped. He was finer than I remembered.

"You must want a fly to go in there." She snickered before yelling, "Hey, Denim!"

A grin spread across his chestnut colored face as he walked across the street and into our yard.

"What's good, EJ!" He trained his black orbs on me. "I had to come over here and make sure I'm seeing right!"

A nervous laugh escaped my lips. "Yeah, it's me."

We stared at each other until EJ cleared her throat.

"Uh, Ms. Roz told me she was leaving." He glanced at EJ before I became his focus again. "Just hit me up if y'all need anything, EJ."

"Man, what you doing?!" somebody yelled from his car.

"Man, I'm coming!" He hollered back. "I gotta go, but I'll see y'all later."

"See you later, Denim," EJ said as I sat there like a knot on a log.

My eyes followed him across the street until he disappeared into the house.

Chubby fingers snapped in my face. "Earth to Choc!"

"Why didn't anybody tell me that Denim stays across the street now?"

I know you're wondering why I was all discombobulated. Remember that guy that I mentioned as I strolled down memory lane? I was talking about him.

"For one, you don't live here. For two, we figured that it didn't matter since you were so absorbed in your doctor and life in Cali."

"Well, all of that is over." I doused my rice with sauce and mixed it around.

"How come?" She pulled a crawfish apart and sucked the head. "Oh my God! These are so good!"

"I'm just mentally exhausted. First my relationship started going to shit, and then my career tried to follow suit."

"You'll bounce back better than ever."

"I hope so, EJ." I sighed.

"And I admire you. I wish I was gifted like that. Then I wouldn't have to spend my days shelving cans of green peas at Wal-Mart."

"Girl, you do not wanna be like me, feeling lost and just drifting. You live a peaceful, simple life. Be thankful."

She fixed her doe eyes on me. "Maybe you're not lost. Maybe it's the universe placing you where you need to be."

***

I had no clue where I was going as I pushed a shopping cart, or a buggy if you're using southern terms, through Winn-Dixie. I'd decided to do a little browsing and snack shopping while EJ feigned an illness at the Urgent Care center across the parking lot. Big bright red poinsettia arrangements caught my eye as I traipsed along.

Those are beautiful! I should get two to take to Brandon. Brandon- he's not here anymore. I'll never see him again in this life.

It's crazy how grief is. You could hold it together and cope for years, but one little image, smell, or place could bring you all the way back down again.

"Ma'am, are you alright?" A bald white guy placed his hand on my shoulder.

"Huh?"

He stepped away, probably unsure if I was batshit crazy. "You're standing in one spot, and you're crying."

I raised my hand and felt the moisture on my face. "Oh, I didn't realize. Sir, I'm not crazy. It's the holiday season, and it's nearing the anniversary of my older brother's death. I'm having a moment."

"I'm sorry to hear that, and I definitely understand. What's your name?"

"Aaliyah."

"I'll be sure to mention it in my prayers." He gave my back a soothing pat.

"I appreciate it."

I placed two floral arrangements in the cart and walked aimlessly towards the rear of the store.

***

Just before dusk, I lugged my belongings inside and into my old room. The full sized bed and the bookshelf were in the same spot, but my mom had changed the color scheme. I flopped down on the bed and yawned loudly. Suddenly, a blast of cold air sent a chill down my spine.

"EJ, cut the air off! What's wrong with you?!" I shouted.

She stuck her head into the doorway. "The air isn't on. This happens very frequently around here, so you might as well get used to it."

"Mama must have cracks in the floors then," I reasoned.

"Girl, ain't no cracks in here. That's just Brandon." She grinned. "Hey, Bran! You happy to see Choc?!"

"Are you scared to be in here by yourself?"

"No," I answered.

"Good because I'm about to take a shower."

***

While EJ showered, I headed to the kitchen to reheat my crawfish. I poured them into a large bowl and microwaved them for a minute. The steam that emitted as I carried them over to the couch opened up my sinuses. I plopped down in front of the large flat screen TV mounted on the wall and picked up the remote, browsing until I found a Christmas movie. Figuring the crawfish had cooled enough, I picked one up, pulled it apart, and sucked the head. The spices flew down my throat and caused me to sputter and choke. Mr. Chang must've enlisted Satan to help boil them. I spotted a half empty water bottle on the end table. Not caring whose lips had been on it, I picked it up and started chugging.

EJ entered the room, hooting in laughter. "Them crawfish are not that hot!"

"Yes... they... are!" My tongue hung out of my mouth like a dog on a hot day. "Whew!"

"Let me find out you ain't a Louisiana girl no more!" She sat beside me and grabbed the bowl.

"You can have them." I got up to grab another bottle of water from the fridge. "I'm going to get a bottle of water. You want one?"

"Yeah."

I watched in amazement as EJ chomped down like the heat was nothing. Shaking my head, I headed into the kitchen.

***

EJ put down a pillow and laid her head in my lap. I cradled her face the way I would when she was just a little girl.

"EJ, why didn't you go with mama? You were gonna be alone for Christmas."

"Her boyfriend did invite me. Even offered to fly me out on Christmas Eve, but I'm just not in the mood to be around a bunch of folks that I don't know. Plus this gives me a break from mama. She acts like I'm two instead of twenty with her smothering," she responded.

"You're the only one that she had here with her. She doesn't mean any harm."

"I know, but what were you gonna do for Christmas if I wasn't here?"

"I don't know." I shrugged. "Lock myself in here and look crazy until y'all came back."

"Or spent Christmas cuddling with Denim."

"No, ma'am!" I exclaimed.

"Why not? He was happy to see you."

I exhaled loudly. "He was just shocked. I don't think Denim likes me like that anymore. It's just a lot..."

"Well, that ain't what I saw today. Plus, I don't think he has a girlfriend, and you're single." She smiled slyly. "How long are you staying here?"

"I'm not sure, but I really don't have anywhere else to go right now," I admitted. "I gotta figure something out."

"What happened with you and the doctor? He was so fine."

"EJ, men can be so perfect until they feel like they got you. He slipped that engagement ring on my finger, and then he changed. We had a big blowup last night, and he basically let me know how he really felt. He assumes that I'm jealous of him and his career because..." I made quotations with my fingers. "I have nothing going for myself. You know, all I ever asked for was some of his time, and he couldn't even do that."

She rolled her eyes. "That nigga must be crazy! Has he called and tried to get you to come back?"

"He's still at work and doesn't know that I'm gone. I left him a note."

"I can just imagine his face when he sees it!" She snickered.

"Knowing Calvin, he probably doesn't care." I yawned loudly. "I'm kinda tired. I better go get cleaned up, so I can go to bed."

She raised up. "Aww, Choc! It's only 8:30!"

"I know, but it's been a long day."

***

EJ was curled up fast asleep on the other side of my bed when I entered the room.

"Got the nerve to talk about me, but look at her." I chuckled while sliding underneath the covers.

I snuggled up close to her and inhaled her scent until I fell asleep.

Chapter 4

The crowing of a rooster roused me from my sleep.

"Oops! Sorry about that!" EJ apologized as she quieted her phone's alarm. "I have to get ready for work."

I sat upright and pushed my back against the headboard. "It's ok. What time do you get off?"

"Six."

"Oh."

When I came here, I hadn't thought about EJ having to work. Now I had no clue what I'd do with myself for nine hours.

"When is your next day off?" I asked.

"Girl, I'm not off until Christmas Eve. The store's been busy as hell."

"Aww man," I pouted. "I guess I'll have to find something to do to occupy my alone time."

I also had to find a way to return my rental to New Orleans by the weekend. I refused to pay the outrageous fees of dropping it at another location.

She pointed towards the window and into the direction of Denim's house.

"Don't start!" I fussed.

"Ok,ok!" She tittered. "I'm about to put on a pot of coffee and brush my teeth. You want some?"

"Sure." I stood up to head into one of the bathrooms to get myself together.

***

I sat in one of the porch chairs with my cup of coffee, waving goodbye to EJ. The breeze felt amazing against my skin, but I knew the cool temp would quickly fade as the day went on. Here winter temps were in the mid to lower sixties, unless it was rainy or a cold front moved through. Denim's front door opened slightly, and I jumped up, splashing hot coffee on my hand.

"Shit!" I hissed.

I didn't want him to see me with my hair tied, nightshirt on, and nipples to the wind.

I made my way to the kitchen and gazed out the window through the small slit in the curtains as he walked towards his car. He paused and glanced in the direction of the house like he could feel me watching before climbing inside and pulling off. After pouring the remainder of the coffee down the sink's drain, I headed into the bedroom to find something to wear.

During the drive here yesterday, I noticed a couple of new food spots and a shopping mall a few towns down, so I was gonna double back and check it out.

***

My phone rang with a call from Apryl. I slid the icon and connected the phone to the speakers of the car. "Hello?"

"Hey! What you doing, girl? I'm off today. You wanna meet for drinks?" she jabbered in her nasally voice.

"If I was in Cali, I would've loved to," I replied.

"Where are you? I saw Cal this morning before I got off, and he didn't say anything about you being gone. He was acting weird though."

"I'm at home, in Louisiana."

"When are you coming back?"

"I don't know if I'm ever coming back to stay."

She gasped. "You and Cal broke up?!"

"Yes, but I ain't trippin'." I honked my horn at a careless driver.

"Why?! Do you know how many women are after that man?!"

"And they can have him."

"I think you guys should try to work it out. He has a good job, he takes care of you, and he didn't wait years to ask for your hand in marriage. Men like him are rare, Choc."

"Just taking care of me financially doesn't cut it. I can pay bills and buy things for myself." The fact that Apryl acted as if Calvin was some sort of precious gem pissed me off. "I wish him well, and I hope he finds someone who is fine with just that."

"Aww, Choc..." she groaned.

"Apryl, I gotta go." I hung up without giving her a chance to say anything else.

"Fuck, Calvin!" I mumbled while scrolling through my playlist.

He hadn't bothered to contact me, and I knew he'd realized that I was gone by now. He most likely was just as tired of me as I was of him.

Pushing Calvin all the way out of my mind, I clicked on Rihanna's "Watch n' Learn", adjusted the volume, and gyrated in my seat.

***

Mariah Carey's "All I Want For Christmas Is You" floated from the speakers as I pushed my cart towards Ross' handbags section. Some cute Betsey Johnson purses caught my eye, so I grabbed one for me and one for EJ. I kept it moving towards the clothing items, where I found a couple of cute cardigans and jeans. Then I moved towards the back of the store to the home goods section. There were so many Christmas decorations that I could use to spruce up the front porch.

I began grabbing things and piling them into the cart. "That'll give me something to do since tomorrow is the day that..."

***

My phone rang as I struggled to push the heavy cart to the car, so I stopped to answer it.

"Hello?" I heaved.

"Choc, where you at? I came home for lunch, and you not here!" EJ exclaimed.

"I didn't want to just sit at home, so I took a ride and did some shopping. I got you some stuff."

"Thank you, but Choc, you don't have to keep spending your money on me. I already have a million packages from you underneath the Christmas tree."

"Shut up, lil girl!" I scoffed. "You don't tell me what to do with my money. Anyway, how's work going so far?"

She kissed her teeth. "It's going. I almost had to bless an old lady out though. That's another reason why I hate the holidays, too many ignorant folks coming through!"

"Just keep your cool, EJ," I advised. "No sense in you getting ignorant too."

"I know..." she sighed. "So listen, I just sat some gravy chops out."

I chuckled. "You hinting around for me to cook tonight?"

"Please... I missed your cooking."

"I gotcha, girlie."

"Yesss!" she cheered. "Well, let me go scrounge around and find something to eat. I'll see you later. Love you."

"Love you too." I smiled before ending the call.

***

I selected a playlist and got to work on our meal for the night. The sliced onions burned the hell out of my eyes. I washed and dried my hands before opening the window above the sink. Denim's bass knocked as he pulled into his driveway. Biting my lip, I observed him like a hawk as his long slightly bowed legs carried him up his front steps and inside.

"Denim, Denim, Denim..."

I had no idea what his relationship status was now, but I could almost guarantee that a specimen that fine belonged to someone. I'd thought about him a lot over the years, every day for the first year and a half of my life in Cali and frequently after that. I know I messed up and added hurt on top of hurt when I left. He completely cut me out of his life, and I eventually moved on with Calvin or tried to.

Exhaling loudly, I tore my eyes from across the street.

***

"This is so good!" EJ exclaimed. "Better than mama's, but don't tell her I said that."

"Thank you." I laughed as she finished up her second helping of food.

"You should fix Denim a plate and take it to him."

My eyes ballooned. "Girl, what?! I'm not going over there!"

"Choc, why you acting like that all of a sudden?" Her face scrunched. "You getting on my nerves!"

"Acting like what?!"

"Like you don't know him no more! What is wrong with you?!" She got up and stormed into the kitchen. "I'mma fix it and take it to him myself!"

I scurried to the kitchen window and watched her strut across the street with the plate in her hand. He opened the door, shirtless, after she knocked twice.

"Damn..." I mumbled.

The window was still raised, so I could hear everything her loud mouth was saying.

"Hey, big bro!"

"What's up, EJ! Whatchu got?!"

"Choc cooked this, but her ass is too scared to bring it over. So here I am!" She passed him the plate as he laughed.

"Thank ya. Tell Choc's fine ass that I ain't gon' bite."

"I will, but I bet her nosy ass is right there in that window."

I dropped down to the hardwood floor like the roof was on fire as his narrowed eyes peered towards the kitchen window.

EJ returned, clucking. "Big chicken, where you at?!"

"I'm right here, and leave me alone!" I walked back into the living room with my arms folded.

"Denim called you fine and said that he won't bite unless you want him to."

"That is not what he said with yo lying crazy ass!"

Her phone rang, interrupting her shenanigans.

"Hey, ma!" she answered. "I'm ok. I kinda miss your aggravating behind."

"I miss you too!" I heard mama laugh. "What have you and your sister been doing?"

"Oohwee! What haven't we been doing?! Your house has been full of hot boys for two days straight!" EJ snickered.

Mama smacked her lips. "Whatever, girl! Let me speak to your sister."

"Alright. Love you, ma!"

"Love you too, crazy!" She laughed.

EJ handed me the phone. "I'm about to go take a bath. Would you put my phone on the charger when y'all finish talking?"

I nodded.

"Hey, mama!" I smiled. "How are you?"

"I'm alright, I guess. How are you?"

"I'm actually doing better than I thought I would. I'm not sure about tomorrow though."

She sighed. "Me too. I'm definitely dreading tomorrow, and I'm now wishing I could be at home with my girls, especially you. I'm not too worried about EJ. I don't think anything fazes that crazy girl. She swears she sees Brandon in the house all the time."

"She probably does, but I don't want you worrying about me. I'll be fine. We'll be fine. We'll get through tomorrow like we've gotten through it for the last couple of years." Crazy how I could tell her something that I wasn't too sure of myself.

Chapter 5

My eyes popped open at seven a.m. and I began what felt like a dream or out of body experience. On autopilot, I brushed my teeth and then made grits, sausage, toast, and coffee. After tinting our plates with foil to keep the food warm, I headed to EJ's room.

I shook her gently. "EJ, wake up so you can eat breakfast."

"Ok... What time is it?" she grumbled while throwing her covers back.

"Fifteen minutes til eight." As she headed towards the bathroom, I began making her bed.

***

EJ watched me closely as we finished up breakfast. "Are you alright? I can call in and stay here with you."

"You don't have to do all that. I'm fine."

"Are you sure?" She eyed me skeptically.

"Yes, EJ. I'm sure. I don't want you to worry about me."

"What are you gonna do while I'm gone?" she quizzed.

"Decorate the porch, try to write a little, and think of a Christmas dinner menu," I responded.

"Well, I'm going to check on you throughout the day, and I'll bring you lunch from this new soul food restaurant."

"Thank you, babydoll." I shot her a small smile. "I appreciate it."

***

Deciding that now would be the perfect time to visit Brandon's grave, I grabbed the two floral arrangements and walked down the street to the cemetery. I hadn't been on this end of the road since the day we'd laid him to rest, and a lot had changed. Dead leaves and fallen tree limbs still lined the street from a recent hurricane, and the majority of the houses and mobile homes were abandoned and falling apart. This definitely wasn't the lively street that it once was.

I was out of breath and had to pause to remove my cardigan before continuing through the second entrance of the graveyard. Brandon's resting place was tucked in a back corner, giving his visitors just the right amount of privacy. My chest tightened as I approached the silver metallic burial vault.

After finding a place to put the flowers amongst the others that were already there, I looked at the numerous pictures of him that were printed onto the top of the custom made vault. My eyes swam with tears as I began to feel weak with emotions. I needed to sit down, so I settled on the cool damp grass in front of the grave.

Everything replayed in my mind as if it'd just happened. Him texting me on his lunch break for the last time. The agony of not knowing where he was for two days. The police knocking on our door saying that they believed they'd found him. Our mother being so distraught that she had to be hospitalized. Me having to go view crime scene photos and identify him. Brandon's brown eyes staring into nothingness. The bruising of his light brown face and knuckles, indicating that he'd put up a fight. The bullet hole in his head surrounded by congealed blood. Those stupid muthafuckas took his life over material things. Material things! This was the worst thing I'd ever experienced in my twenty-four years of living. Not only was I mourning the loss of my brother, but he was also one of my best friends. Why did something so horrific have to happen to him? It wasn't fair, and there were plenty of days where I'd go from trusting God to questioning Him.

They'd caught the perpetrators and sentenced them all to life, but it wasn't good enough for me. They were still living and breathing. Their families could see them and talk to them. All we had were thoughts of what could've been and this big block of concrete that sat before me. I wept as the wind scattered the dead leaves around me.

Somehow, I gathered myself and trudged back towards the house. I was in such a daze that I didn't bother to check who was calling my phone before answering it.

"Choc, Calvin looks so sad! I think you should call him," Apyrl blurted the second the call connected.

"Calvin looks sad?! Ha! Bitch, it's the anniversary of my brother's death, and I can't get a "Hi, Choc! I just want you to know that I'm thinking of you today" or a "Hi, Choc! How are you doing mentally today?"

"I'm sorry. I completely forgot."

"And it's not just today, Apryl! You never once showed concern for me since I left. It's always Calvin this and Calvin that! I understand that you introduced us, but goddamn! You really need to get you some fucking business outside of what we had going on! Matter of fact, since he's so perfect, why don't you get with him?! Give him a little pussy since you seem to be feeling him more than I am!" I lashed out.

Her voice quivered as if she were going to cry. "I'm just gonna hang up since you're talking crazy and acting like someone that I don't even know right now."

"Good, and do us both a favor by not calling back," I spat.

My body was ready to shut down by the time I made it home. I sent EJ a text letting her know that I was going back to bed, slipped off my shoes, and sprawled out on top of the bedding.

***

Light taps on the side of my face caused me to stir in my sleep. "Choc! Choc, wake up!"

I rubbed the sleep from my eyes, trying to clear my vision.

"Brandon?!" I gasped before throwing my arms around him.

His body felt solid and warm, the way it would if he were still alive.

"What are you doing here? I thought you were..." A lone tear cascaded down my cheek.

He used his thumb to brush it away. "Yes, I'm physically gone, but I wanted you to see me. We gotta talk about what you got going on."

"Ok." I nodded. "But first, I just wanna touch you. It's been so long."

He laughed as I grabbed his hands, caressed his face, and felt his locs before wrapping my arms around him tightly again.

"How about we just hold each other while we talk?" he suggested, rubbing my back.

"Ok."

"I'm glad you're back, Choc. The family ain't been the same since you left. They need you here."

"But, Bran, life is so hard here without you. I don't know if I want to stay." I inhaled, breathing in his familiar scent.

"It's gonna get easier. Their love and support will help you heal. Plus y'all will never be without me. I'm always around. Will you please stay? For me?" He pried my arms away so that he could look into my eyes.

"Yes, I'll stay."

"Good." His eyes sparkled as he pulled me back into his arms.

I rested my head on his shoulder as he continued, "I need you to do one more thing for me."

"What's that?" I asked.

"Quit being scared and have a talk with my boy. Patch things up."

"Alright, I will."

"I can't stay long, but before I go, I just want you to know that I'm proud of you and all of your accomplishments. Keep pushing."

"Thank you, Brandon. I love you." I raised my head and kissed his cheek.

He didn't feel as solid anymore; he was slowly fading away.

"I love you too. I gotta go, but I'll be back to see you soon."

***

When I opened my eyes, for real this time, my arms were wrapped around myself, and my room smelled like him. After sitting on the edge of the bed for a minute, I glanced at the wall clock and realized that I'd slept the majority of the day away. My stomach growled, letting me know that I needed to fill it with something.

I entered the kitchen to find a plate of shrimp, tomato, and okra stew, green beans, and a small container of banana pudding with a note from EJ saying that I was sleeping so well that she decided not to wake me. After heating the food, I sat at the small kitchen table and ate while checking my phone. There were messages from my mama telling me that she was thinking about me, that she loved me, and how everything would be alright. I hit the camera icon to FaceTime her.

"Hershey Kiss!" she greeted me. "You finally woke up!"

"Yes, ma'am."

"Are you ok? I've been worried about you,"

"I was a mess, but I'm better now." The thought of my encounter with Brandon brought a smile to my face. "How are you?"

"I'm dog tired. I been going and going all day. These people around here stay in the streets." She turned her attention to the person sitting beside her. "I'm talking to my daughter."

She shifted her focus back to me. "These people are nosy as hell, Choc!"

Her phone was snatched, and another woman's round face appeared. "Hey, darlin'! Damn, you are a beautiful chocolate thang! I'm Amy, your mom's sis-in-law."

"Hi, Amy! Nice to meet you!" I grinned.

"Listen, your mama was just in the middle of telling me about your books, and I wanna know where I can purchase them."

"Amazon, Barnes and Noble, Books A Million, or Wal-Mart." I rattled off.

"Thank you! After we leave here, I'm going to buy as many copies as I can and gift them to some of my friends."

"Wow! Thank you for your support!" I beamed.

"Be blessed and continue to keep up the good work, baby!" She grinned before mama came back into view.

"Girl, I been slanging your books like dope! Even talking to people that look like they can't read!" Mama laughed. "Check your sales because a lot of Andrew's family has ordered paperback versions of your books."

"Thank you, ma! I appreciate it."

"You're welcome, but listen, baby, our food is coming out. I'll call you back later."

"Alright, ma. Love ya!"

"Love you too, sweetie!" She blew me a kiss before hanging up.

***

As I finished devouring the last spoonful of banana pudding, my publisher called.

"Hi, Sammie!" I answered.

"Hi, Chocolata!" she exclaimed in her thick New York accent. "I got some good news!"

"Lord knows I could use it! Lay it on me!"

"Well..." Samantha drawled. "There's been a big influx in your book sales this week from hardcopies to ebooks. You need to jump back on social media and ride that wave. Post your favorite excerpts. Post pictures on your personal and business pages, you know readers love when they can get to know their favorite authors outside of books. And lastly, work on something to put out soon. Another book of poetry, anything. I see a major comeback on the horizon."

"Yes, ma'am. I'll get on it tomorrow." A genuine smile stretched across my face. "Thank you! You don't know how much I needed this news, especially on today."

"Oh, I did! I remember what today is. That's why I called instead of emailing you."

"Aww, thanks! Sammie, you do have a heart!" I joked.

"Of course, I do!" she chuckled. "And don't tell your pen brothers and sisters this, but you're my favorite."

"Aww!"

"I gotta go, but I'll be in touch soon."

"Ok. Thanks for calling me. Talk to you later." I ended the call with renewed hope.

There were about two hours of daylight left when I decided to decorate the porch.

"First, I should start with the easy stuff, like replacing these throw pillows on the furniture with these Christmas ones." I talked to myself.

After completing that, I decided to start on the door. I had these little hooks that I could stick on there to hang a wreath, but I needed something to stand on in order to hang the other stuff. I didn't have a stepstool, so a chair would have to do. I went and dragged one out of the kitchen.

"I know you fucking lying to me," I cussed as the hook and the wreath crashed to the floor for the second time. "I bought all of these things and probably can't hang none of this stuff up with them."

A laugh I knew all too well rang out behind me.

My face flushed as I turned around. "How long have you been standing there?"

"A good lil minute." His teeth gleamed white against his brown skin. "I was actually coming to see how you were doing."

"I'm ok. How about you?" My eyes raked his handsome features.

"I'm making it."

"That's good. Denim, if you don't mind, will you help me with this?"

He climbed the few steps onto the porch. "Sure. Let me see what you got."

I passed him the wreath and the hook.

"This here ain't gon' work, but lucky for you, I have a wreath hanger at my house. What else you got?"

I retrieved the gutter hooks. "The guy at the store told me to get these to hang the lights."

"And how were you gonna hang lights without a ladder?"

"Shit, I have no idea." Heat tinged my ears. "We'll just skip that part."

"I'm just messing with you!" He laughed. "I'll be right back."

***

I perched up in one of the chairs while Denim did the majority of the work, hanging lights, garland, and red bows.

"Choc, you owe me for this shit!" He peeled his t-shirt from his sweaty frame, putting his tatted up torso on full display.

"Damn, Denny..." Realizing I'd spoken aloud and called him by a pet name, my hand flew over my mouth. Thank God he didn't hear me. "What I owe you?"

"You gotta give me your number and chill with me this week," he responded.

"That's all?"

"Yeah, that's all." He finished hanging the last bow. "Go plug everything up and come down here to see how it looks."

"It looks good." I stood beside him in the yard and admired the decorations. "Thank you, Denim."

"You're welcome."

"You wanna come inside and let me feed you?" I offered.

"Hell yeah!" He grinned. "That rice and gravy was so good yesterday."

"We got some left over. Come on." I grabbed his hand and led him inside to the kitchen.

***

I took a seat across from him at the table. "I appreciate you not being weird towards me."

His thick brows knitted. "Why would I be weird towards you?"

"Because of the way I left. I know you were mad at me, and you had every right to be."

"Mad? No, Choc."

"But, Denim, the last time I talked to you, you hung up in my face!" I blurted. "And then you blocked me!"

"I was more hurt than anything, and I shouldn't have done that. The first couple of weeks after your brother died, you started getting distant. Then you waited the day before your flight to tell me that you were going to California and that you weren't coming back. In my mind, I felt like you was saying fuck me and whatever I thought we had."

"I'm sorry, Denim. I would never do anything to intentionally hurt you. I was just lost in a world of pain, and didn't quite know how to handle it." My voice cracked. "I never shared this with anybody else, but I'm the one that saw the damage before the morticians worked their magic, and that shit scarred me so badly. The nightmares. Do you know what it's like to dread sleeping while also hating to be awake? I felt like I was losing my mind, so I used my education as an escape and got away from here. I went through hell even in California; intense therapy sessions, taking antidepressants and prescribed sleep aids."

I got up to grab a napkin to wipe my eyes.

"I'm sorry you had to experience that, and I'm sorry there was nothing I could do to help." My body relaxed as he wrapped his arms around me from behind.

"It's ok. I'm alright now. Just do me a favor and keep what I just shared with you to yourself."

"Of course," he replied. "I'm glad we had this conversation."

"Me too." I let out a deep breath. "You should go eat your food before it gets cold, and I need to get myself together before EJ gets-."

Hearing her open the front door, Denim stepped back.

"What's going on here?!" She stood at the kitchen's entrance with one brow cocked. "Why is he naked?! Let me find out!"

"Will you shut up?!" I scolded. "So doggone embarrassing."

"Hey, EJ!" Denim laughed.

"Hey, Denim! I know I usually give you a hug, but I'm kinda rank."

"EJ!" I frowned.

She held up her hands. "I'll see you later."

I shook my head. "I don't know what's wrong with my sister. It seems like the older she gets the crazier she becomes."

"EJ is just being EJ. She don't mean no harm." He chuckled.

"I know."

"Is it cool if I take my plate home?"

"Sure. Let me get some foil and wrap it up for you."

His eyes followed me as I tore off a piece and carried it to where his plate rested on the table.

I tucked a loose curl behind my ear. "What?"

His gaze didn't waiver. "I missed you, and I'm glad you came back."

"I missed you too."

After wrapping up his food, I led him out onto the porch.

"Thank you for coming over."

"You're welcome, but I'mma need part of what you owe me before I go." He flashed his pearly whites as he slid his phone from his back pocket.

I keyed my number in and passed it back.

"I'll text you later tonight." He leaned forward and pressed his lips to my forehead.

"Ok..."

I felt lighter as I watched his long legs carry him across the road to his house.

***

"What happened between you and Denim today? He was standing mighty close to you when I walked in." EJ stood in the bedroom doorway as I rummaged through my bags for some pajamas.

"Nothing. He came over and helped me decorate the house, and then I fed him."

"Oh. Well, that's progress, I guess."

"Why are you so doggone nosy? I need to start getting in your business."

"What you wanna know? I hide nothing!" She came in and sat on the edge of the bed.

"You and Chris together today or nah?" I asked.

Chris was the guy EJ'd been with since she was in middle school. Even though they loved each other, they were both crazy, and in the past, their spats would get volatile. One while, mama made EJ quit talking to him.

"Girl, yeah. We haven't been getting along lately, so he better buy me a good Christmas present to make it right."

"You are a mess! Oh yeah, here. I forgot to give this to you yesterday." I passed her a plastic bag with the Betsey Johnson purse, cardigans, jeans, and one of the Chanel bags I brought here with me.

"Oooh, Chanel!" she squealed. "I know this didn't come from Ross!"

"Nope, but I want you to have it. I hope you like your other stuff."

Her smile spread wider as she pulled out each item. "I love them! Thank you, Choc!"

I gathered my pajamas and terry cloth headband. "You're welcome, babydoll. I'm about to go take a bath."

"Ok. I'm kinda tired, so I'll probably be asleep when you finish."

"Well, good night, and I love you." I walked over and kissed her forehead.

***

After running the water nice and hot, I lit the vanilla scented candles that sat on the countertop. The water's temperature instantly relaxed all of my muscles as I sank down into the tub. Basking in comfort, I closed my eyes for a few minutes until the ping of my phone sounded. I clicked on the message from Denim.

Denim: Hey, what you doing?

Me: Nothing. What you doing?

Denim: Thinking about you

Me: Aww. Really?

Denim: Yes ma'am. What you got planned for tomorrow?

Me: Absolutely nothing

Denim: You wanna go fishing with me in the morning?

Me: Sure.

Denim: Be ready to roll at 7

Me: Ok. See you then

Denim: See you then

I placed the phone on the toilet seat before bathing and getting out of the tub.

***

I dug around the top of the closet until I found my old rubber boots. Now I had to find something to put on. I threw an oversized t-shirt and a pair of black leggings onto the chair in the corner of the room. Yawning loudly, I crawled into bed with Denim on the brain.

Chapter 6

When I stepped outside to meet Denim, the red pickup truck with the small boat attached was the last thing I expected.

"Good morning!" he greeted.

"Morning!" I responded, closing the door and reaching for the seatbelt. "I thought when you said fishing you meant sitting on the bank of a pond like we used to do."

"Naw. I figured we could ride out to Manchac and see what's biting. That's cool with you?"

"Yeah." I nodded.

"First, we gon' stop and get us some breakfast."

***

The aroma of the freshly baked pastries was heavenly as we entered the donut shop. I made a beeline to the coffee maker for a large cup of Community coffee with chicory while Denim grabbed a bottle of orange juice from the cooler. I listened to him place an order as I added a few teaspoons of sugar and extra cream.

"Good morning! Can I get two ham and cheese croissants, one lemon and one cream filled donut?"

I smiled at the fact that he still remembered what I liked.

"Is that all, along with your juice?" the clerk asked.

With his thumb, he gestured in my direction. "You can add her coffee on there too."

After paying for our food, he handed me the bag with my donuts.

"Thank you, Denim." I grinned. "I see you still remember my favorites."

"I remember everything about you, Choc."

He walked ahead of me to the truck and opened the passenger door, making sure I was settled comfortably inside before closing it.

Once my seat belt was fastened, I tucked two of the brown napkins into the collar of my shirt and went in on the donuts.

"Damn, you ain't playing around, huh?" Denim teased. "You eating like them niggas in the plant."

"I ain't had nothing like this in a long time, so I don't care what you say." I took a second bite of the lemon filled one and moaned.

"Don't look like it."

"What's that supposed to mean?" I scowled.

"Relax. I didn't mean it in a bad way." His eyes swept over my frame for a split second then darted back to the road ahead. "It's just them curves that you came back with…"

"Oh…"

"Yep. You fine as hell."

I pivoted towards the window in an attempt to conceal the rosiness that crept up my cheeks.

"So tell me about your life in Cali."

"Ain't nothing to tell. I'm a homebody that writes books."

"You know, some of them scenes in your first ones seem mighty familiar to me." He smirked.

I gasped. "You read them?"

They were heavily Denim inspired, and some of the spicy scenes mirrored real life.

"Every one and loved them too. What's it like creating that type of stuff? What's the process?"

"I didn't think you'd be interested in that kind of thing."

"I'm interested in whatever has to do with you." He turned his brown eyes on me as we stopped at a light.

"Oh. Well, you know how it is when you watch a good movie and get lost in it?"

He nodded as I continued.

"It's like that, except your mind is the screen. You watch, and then you write down what you see. The only difference is with a television screen it's easy to turn things on and off. In your mind, it's hard to pause it sometimes, and you can't concentrate on anything else until you get it on paper."

"What about poetry?"

"Poetry is fueled by pure emotion, or at least mine is. A lot of those poems in my book of poetry were written when I was eighteen or nineteen, when I was in a very happy, raw emotional state."

"When we first started..." he mumbled.

"Yep, and I haven't penned a poem in years. Now tell me about what you been up to."

"I ain't been up to nothing. I go to work and bring my ass right back home."

"So you don't do anything else?" I raised a perfectly trimmed brow.

"Nope, unless one of my people calls me to help them with something. Other than that, I'm inside."

"Denim, you are too- You mean to tell me that you spend the majority of your time at home alone? You don't have anybody that you're seeing or anybody to scratch that itch?"

"This is all I got." He held up his right hand. "Now, what you got going on? You chillin' with me today ain't gon' cause problems, is it?"

"I don't have nothing going on."

"I thought you was engaged to a doctor." He unwrapped his croissant and took a bite.

"I was, but not anymore."

"Oh..."

I knew by the expression on his face that he was in deep thought.

"Denim, what you thinking about?"

"Nothing," he responded before taking another bite of his breakfast.

Deciding not to press him, I wiped my hands and reached up to adjust the radio's volume.

***

"Choc, get in the boat!" Denim chortled as I stood there scared to death.

"This is a lot of water, and I don't know if this can hold us, the cooler, and whatever we catch."

"Yes, it can. The boat ain't that small. If you scared, you can sit close to me." He held his hand out for me to grab.

"But won't that make the weight unbalanced?"

"It's not like a seesaw, Choc. One end isn't gonna rise up. Come on. I'm not gonna let nothing happen to you."

I took a deep breath, grabbed his hand, and stepped into the boat.

"Sit right here while I steer out a little further," he instructed.

"Ok," I replied in a shaky voice.

***

After being out on the water for a while, I'd gotten comfortable and was able to really take in the scenery. The mossy trees, the lily pads concealing areas of the dark water, the small houses on stilts. It was gritty and rough, but there was something magnificent about simple Louisiana living.

"It's beautiful out here," I commented.

"I know. I figured we could just enjoy the scenery and the vibes even if we don't catch anything," Denim stated.

Just then, I felt a tug on my line.

"I think I got something! It feels heavy!" I began to slowly reel it in until the fish was visible above the water.

"Looks like a largemouth bass. You doing good." We exchanged poles so he could remove it from the hook.

"Looks like you got something too!" I exclaimed, straining to reel in his line.

He threw my fish into a cooler and grabbed the pole. The fish at the end of the line was humongous. It slipped from his hands as he tried to remove the hook and flipped wildly around the boat.

"Ahh!" I screamed in terror.

He finally got a grip on it. "Choc, chill out! I got it!"

"I think I'll just let you fish while I enjoy the scenery." I grabbed my small backpack and went to the opposite end of the boat.

"So you just gon' leave me hanging?"

"I'm just gonna take a little break. I'll try my luck again before we leave."

Once semi-comfortable, I unzipped my bag and grabbed my phone and my AirPods. My eyes swept over the water and the trees as soft RnB entered my ears. Lastly, they landed on Denim, who paid me no mind. His muscles flexed as he pulled up another fairly large fish. I began to feel something I hadn't felt in a long time, inspired. Not to write a story, but a poem. I grabbed the small notebook and pen from the backpack. The ball point black gel pen moved smoothly across the college ruled paper. When I finally looked up, Denim was watching me closely.

"What you writing?"

"Huh?" I turned my music off.

"What you writing?" he repeated.

"Oh. A poem."

"Can I read it?"

"No." I clutched the notebook close to my chest as if he would try to snatch it.

He shrugged. "Fine then."

"I'll let you read it one day."

"Well, are you feeling alright?" He observed me with eyes full of concern. "I know you said your emotions fuel your poetry."

"I'm not sad," I clarified. "It's not that kind of poem."

It was the kind of poem that described how the rays of the sun graced the melanin of his skin, how it brought out the brown tones in his eyes that you'd think were pitch black in the shade, how the waves in his hair were just as deep and rippled as the body of water that we sat in the middle of.

"Welp, since I can't read your poem, I guess I can't show you these beautiful pictures that I took." He grinned slyly.

"What pictures?" I stood up abruptly, causing the boat to rock and scaring myself for a second.

He passed me his phone, and my eyes landed on an off guard of me gazing off into the distance. The top of my pen rested against my chin as I thought deeply about how to translate my thoughts on paper. The next one was me concentrating on what was on the paper. These shots were better than the ones that I'd paid professionals for.

"These are beautiful! You gotta send them to me. I could use them on my social media pages."

"I will. Just remind me."

"And if you don't mind, can I snap a few shots of you?"

"Why you wanna take pictures of me looking like this?" He frowned.

"Because you're handsome, and I wanna show my readers the inspiration for some of my work. But if you don't want me to, I understand."

"Naw, you can. What you want me to do?"

"Just look at the camera." I held my phone up and snapped three pics. "I'm done."

"You coming back over here to fish or at least just sit by me?"

"Yes." I plopped down beside him on the raised portion of the boat. "Take a selfie with me right quick."

***

At about one o'clock, we headed in to get out of the heat and to find something to eat. He took me to this place called Fat Boy's where he ordered me a Swamp Burger.

"This is so good." I smacked as I savored the last bite. "Thank you for inviting me to come here with you. You made my day. I really missed this." I gestured between us.

"I missed this too. How long are you gonna be down here?"

"I have absolutely no plans to return to Cali anytime soon. It may sound crazy, but I'm back to start anew."

He smiled so wide that I got a glimpse of all thirty-two of his teeth.

"Nothing wrong with starting over."

***

We rode through our hometown to the next town over.

"I gotta take Mr. Percy his truck and his boat and get my car. I hope his crazy ass ain't wreck my shit," Denim said as we made a right turn onto a long rock road.

A double wide mobile home sat up ahead on about an acre of land. There were numerous broken down vehicles in the yard. As we got closer, I saw a man wearing a white tee and suspenders sitting on a swing on the trailer's porch. Denim parked the truck a few feet from the trailer and stepped out.

"Was the fish biting?" the old man asked.

"Oohwee! Was they!" Denim replied, walking over to the passenger side. "I caught enough to share with you. I'll bring them by after I clean them."

He adjusted his glasses as Denim helped me exit the vehicle.

"This is Choc. Choc, this is Mr. Percy," He led me onto the porch. "Mr. Percy is my usual fishing buddy."

"Choc... Brandon's sister?"

"Yep. That's her."

"It's nice to meet you." When I extended my hand, he kissed it. "I see why he told me I couldn't come this morning. You sure are a pretty chocolate thang."

"Aye! Keep your old lips to yourself. Don't be getting fresh with her!" Denim kidded.

"Whatever, boy." Mr. Percy reached into his pocket, tossed Denim his keys, and patted the empty spot beside him. "Come have a seat while Denim unloads the truck."

"I heard a few things about you, young lady." he whispered with a twinkle in his eye.

Swiping at a flyway curl, I whispered back, "Good things I hope."

"You see that boy right there…" He pointed at Denim as he carried our stuff from the truck to his car. "The way he would talk about you… I've never heard him talk that way about anybody else. He called me last night all happy. Happier than he's been in a long time."

Denim walked onto the porch with one of the fishing poles. "Whatever Mr. Percy is telling you is probably a lie. That's all he does."

"Boy, you gets on my damn nerves!" Mr. Percy spat.

I shook my head while laughing at their banter.

"You ready?" Denim asked me.

"Yeah." I rose to my feet. "It was nice meeting you, Mr. Percy."

He peered over the rim of his small lenses. "The pleasure was all mine, sweetheart."

Denim smacked his lips before bending down and pulling him in for a hug.

"I'll be back Sunday to take your truck to the car wash."

"Ok, son. See you Sunday. See you later, Choc." He waved.

***

"Me and Bran used to work with Mr. Percy. He cool, just crazy as hell," Denim said.

"I can tell." I chuckled.

"You need to stop at the store?" he asked while pulling onto the main highway.

"No thank you." The loss of sleep from an early rise began to take a toll on me, causing me to let out a yawn. "Excuse me."

I stared out the tinted window as we crossed the railroad tracks. "I see they redid the library, and my favorite thrift store is still open. Ooh, and they opened up a wing spot."

"Yeah, the library is nice. That wing spot is hit and miss," Denim commented.

"Good to know."

He made a left turn and then another right, turning onto the street in front of the high school.

"There's your favorite place." He pointed.

"They did me bad my freshman year. Painted me out to be loose as a goose. None of the girls liked me."

"Yep, and Brandon stayed whooping ass behind you. Remember he literally beat the piss out of cross eyed David?"

"Yess!" I guffawed. "He shouldn't have lied. I tried to be nice and help his dumb ass study, but he came back to school telling everybody that I sucked his dick."

"And then Ms. Roz..." He busted out laughing.

"She was embarrassing too, coming up to the school as loud and ghetto as ever. *Bring your lil ugly ass here! Apologize to her before I have my son beat yo ass again!*" I cackled. "They put a stop to all rumors though. I wonder how David nem are doing now."

"I saw them at homecoming. Some are doing good, and some of them, life is kicking their ass."

"Yeah, well eventually life begins to kick all our asses," I stated matter of factly.

***

"Well, my debt has been paid." Denim and I stood outside his car. "I guess I'll see you when I see you."

"Damn, it's like that?"

"No, I'm just joking."

His eyes locked onto mine. "Good because I wanna take you out somewhere a little fancier than the bayou."

"I'd like that. Just let me know when." I nibbled on my bottom lip.

"And you don't have to sit at home by yourself while EJ is gone. My next job doesn't start until the middle of next month, so I'll be at home. You can come over or call me if you want some company."

"Ok. I will." My phone started pinging like crazy, receiving delayed messages. "That's my mama. I should go call her."

"Alright. Tell her I said hello."

"Ok." I began to walk towards our yard.

***

"Hey, mama! I'm so sorry. I forgot to text you before I left out this morning, and I didn't have good service out on the water," I stated the minute she picked up.

"It's ok. I called EJ, and she told me where you were."

"Anyway, how are you doing today, ma?" I slipped off my rubber boots near the door before proceeding further into the house.

"I'm good. And you?" She elevated a brow.

"I'm great. Why you looking like that?" I giggled.

"You and Denim. I think you should watch yourself with that."

"Nothing is going on. We went fishing and came home. Oh, and he said to tell you hello."

"I hear ya, girl. Denim is a good young man, and you know how he is or was with you. I just don't want things to get complicated."

"Why would they get complicated? Ma, you doing too much." I chuckled.

"Naw, sista girl! Make sure you don't do too much. You do have a man in California."

"About that, I haven't told you the full story." I sat down Indian style on the hardwood floor. "I left him. That's why I said I was staying here for a while, just until I buy a car and find my own place."

"You can stay with me as long as you want. You already know that."

"Yes, ma'am. I do."

"But happened with you and Calvin?" she asked.

I sighed deeply. "We have different priorities. He's one of those people that focuses solely on their career and misses out on other important things. I, on the other hand, want to get married to a man that makes our relationship a priority and build a family with a strong male presence. I don't want to be a married single mother. I loved Calvin, but we started to lose our connection. I hoped and wished that we could get back right, but the other night I realized that it wasn't going to happen."

"I'm sorry, Choc. It's gonna be alright."

"I know. I'm not sweating it."

"Can I be honest with you, baby?"

"Yes, ma'am." I nodded.

"I wasn't too sure about him in the first place. The age difference. You're twenty-four, and he's thirty-seven. I also thought that y'all moved too fast."

"You never told me that though."

"I didn't really know the man as well as you do, and it wasn't my relationship. All I can do is hope that I taught you girls to know your worth and that you don't have to settle for less than you deserve."

"You did, and I appreciate you for that. Now I'm gonna just focus on my career and jumping back onto the literary scene. I penned a poem today." I smiled.

"That's good, sweetie."

"Roz, you wanna ride to the store with me?!" someone hollered in the background.

"Yeah, give me a minute!" she shouted back, rolling her eyes. "I'm getting sick of these people. I told Andrew that I want to leave early and come home for Christmas because I miss my girls. He agreed that we could leave on Christmas Eve."

"Good. I can't wait to hug you."

"I can't wait to hug you either, but let me go out into the streets. Again."

"Bye, ma! Love you." I laughed.

"Love you too, baby."

After hanging up, I headed to the shower to wash away the smell of outside.

***

"So how was your fishing trip? Did anything interesting happen?" EJ sat at the end of my bed.

"None of your business! You haven't spent ten minutes with me today!" I pretended to pout. "And you look like that Bratz Doll meme!"

She came in from work and dipped right back out, leaving me here by myself.

"I know, and I'm sorry. I had- Chris- uh..." she stammered. "Tell me what happened, Choc! Please!"

"I guess I'll tell you, but before I do, you have to promise that you won't judge me."

"Girl, you know I won't. Now spill it!"

"Ok... Well, we went down to the bayou. There were mossy trees and lily pads all around...." I began.

"I'm not trying to be rude, but I don't give a damn about no trees and all that. Get to the good part!"

"I am. Impatient ass!" I giggled. "Anyway, we were just having regular conversation and waiting for the fish to bite. The sun was beaming, and Denim had gotten hot. So he removed his shirt. The sunlight shining on his tatted chest and arms was so sexy. My panties became wet and my insides started thumping. I wanted him bad."

"Damn..." she mumbled.

"Yeah. I couldn't control myself, so I made a move, and he didn't stop me. He obviously wanted me too."

"What kind of move?!" She bounced her legs in excitement.

"I kissed him and started massaging that snake through his sweats. I needed it. I needed to taste it, so I pulled it out and dropped to my knees."

EJ's mouth hit the floor.

"I sucked, and I licked until he was on the verge of busting. Then he stopped me because he wanted to feel my sugar walls. I removed my boots and bottoms and bent over in the middle of the small boat. Girl, when I tell you Denim put that dick on me! Had me screaming his name. He beat my pussy so bad that if she had eyes, I'm sure she would've been crying. There were houses nearby, but we didn't give a fuck who saw us. You know how they say *"Rock the boat, don't tip the boat over?"* That's exactly what we did!" I grinned slyly.

"You little slut!"

"Wait a minute now! You said you wouldn't judge me!"

"I'm not! That was a compliment. Why that kind of stuff can't happen to me?"

"Oh yeah, I forgot to tell you one more thing."

She leaned forward, ready to soak up all the tea. "What?!"

"I just made all that shit up!" I hollered as her face dropped.

"I hate you!" She scowled.

"I love you too. Are you sleeping in here with me?"

She smacked her lips. "I guess."

Chapter 7

The next day, it rained cats and dogs, but I loved it. After waving goodbye to EJ, I opened up all the curtains, lit some scented candles, selected an RnB playlist, and grabbed my laptop. Wrapped up in my favorite cashmere cardigan, I stretched out on the couch. I decided to go ahead and reactivate my social media accounts before I started on my writing. I posted the off guards that Denim had snapped and captioned them "She's back!". I then went to my kindle app, downloaded my first two releases, and created some kindle quotes. I uploaded them along with the picture I took of Denim and our selfie, captioning them "The Inspo" along with book links. Deciding that those would do for now, I opened up Google Docs and started a brand new story. The ideas started flowing like a waterfall as my fingers glided across the keyboard, and before long I had ten thousand words. I paused momentarily to take a sip of pineapple juice and started up again.

An hour into typing, my eyes and fingers needed a break, so I took the time to check my phone, which I'd silenced. There were messages from Denim, and Apryl. A smile spread across my face as I read his message.

Denim: Good morning I woke up thinking about you.

Me: Good morning I woke up thinking about you too

Then I clicked on Apryl's text.

Apryl: Good morning I just wanted to apologize. I've been a horrible friend, and I'm sorry. I just want you to know that I love you, and I support you in your decision. I'm gonna call you when I get off. Please answer.

Me: Good morning, girlie! I accept your apology, and I love you too.

Exiting my messages, I went to the Amazon app to order matching Christmas outfits for EJ and I, along with the books that I'd promised Shanice. Once my order was confirmed, I got up to get some raisin toast and apple butter.

***

It was beginning to look like a 30K day when Denim texted me again.

Denim: Chocolate what you doing

I texted back without a second thought. **Wanna come over when it slacks up?**

Denim: Sure

Fifteen minutes later, he was knocking on the door.

"It's a vibe in here," he commented, leaving his umbrella in the holder by the door and slipping off his shoes.

"I was having a writing session, but I think I'm done for the day."

He headed over to the couch and took a seat. "Can I read what you got?"

"Only if you promise to give me honest feedback, and I mean brutally honest."

"I don't know how to be anything else but real. Now let me see." He held his hand out as I passed him the laptop.

"I'm about to make myself a turkey sandwich with honey mustard. You want one?" I offered.

"Hell yeah! Look here, Choc, when it comes to food, I'mma always want some."

"Noted." I chuckled as I headed into the kitchen.

I don't know why, but I began to get nervous about him reading what I'd written, especially since I couldn't see his facial expressions.

He probably thinks it's horrible. I thought as I moved about the kitchen.

After making the sandwiches and grabbing two bottled waters, I headed back into the living room. Never taking his eyes away from the computer screen, he reached for his food. As I ate mine, I leaned over slightly, trying to read him, but he wore a poker face. *Damn it!* Needing a good distraction, I picked up my phone and opened up Facebook. People were going crazy and salivating over Denim in the comments. Some were even bold enough to say that they'd fuck the shit out of him. Many were asking if that was my man. *Shid, I wish!* There were thousands of comments and shares, and my nosy behind read every last one of them. I was so busy eating and scrolling that I didn't realize he'd finished reading.

"Mannn..." He blew out.

"What? It's bad? It doesn't make sense? You don't like it?" I blabbered.

He looked me dead in the eyes. "No, I don't like it."

My heart shattered. "Ok... How can I make it better? What don't you like about it?"

"I'm sorry, but I don't think there's nothing you can do to make it better."

"Really? Denim, are you serious?" I fought to hold back my tears. *Maybe my writing career has run its course.*

"Serious as a heart attack," he stated. "I don't like it because I love it."

"Oh my God!" I gasped. "You do? You had me over here about to cry!" I tossed one of the small throw pillows at his head.

"But what's wrong with you? Why is this book so nasty?" He laughed.

"That's what they like." I shrugged.

I stood up to take our plates and turn off the music.

"Whatchu doing? Don't kill the vibe. Let it play."

"Ok…"

Conversation was not needed as we listened to the music while the rain beat down on the roof. That was the thing about Denim and I, we always could connect without words. I swayed and softly sang along with HER as "Comfortable" played and came to an end. It was exactly how I felt. Denim slouched on the sofa with his eyes shut, but I could tell by his breathing that he wasn't asleep. My eyes roved his body from head to toe. His fresh haircut. His thick eyebrows, one with a small slit. His nose that wasn't too wide or too narrow. His thick lips, the bottom one just a tad lighter in color than the top one. His neatly trimmed mustache and beard. The tattoo on his chest that peeked out from the neckline of his wife beater. The large cross on his arm that matched the smaller one on my left leg. The gray sweats, lawd the gray sweats, and my knowledge of what they held. The sounds of Jazmine Sullivan floated through the room, fueling my lustful thoughts.

Got it wetter than the whole Chesapeake Bay

Nothing's stoppin' you

Be the Nia to the hood Larenz Tate

Dive in it (ooh), take your time with it (ooh)

Lil' bowlegged hood nigga with the nine inch (ooh)

Put it in my face

It'd been drafty in here earlier, but not anymore. Feeling myself starting to perspire, I removed my cardigan. His eyes were on me when I glanced up.

"You good?"

"Yeah." I attempted to swallow the basketball sized lump in my throat, forget a golf ball. "Just a little warm. It's this thick cardigan."

His phone rang at just the right moment. I lowered the music's volume and carried my laptop back into my room.

He was on his feet when I returned. "That was Mr. Percy. I gotta go help him with something."

"Ok. Tell him I said hello."

"Choc, what you doing Saturday?" he asked.

"I was gonna take my car back to the rental place when EJ got off," I answered.

"We can do it."

"But it's all the way in New Orleans."

"So? I'll follow you, and we'll go out to eat afterwards."

"Alright." I grinned.

When he finished slipping on his shoes, I walked him out onto the porch. The rain had slacked off into a light drizzle. He opened his arms for me to step into. Embracing me, he placed a kiss on my forehead.

"I'll see you later."

"See you later," I replied.

***

"Spill the beans, bitch! Who is he?" Apryl blurted before I could even say hello.

"What?" I chuckled.

"That guy. The one on your page."

"That's Denim, an old friend. He makes me want to write poetry and shit."

"I see why, and I know what that means." She giggled.

"We have history, and we're reconnecting a little bit. And I don't wanna hear anything about how I just broke up with one man."

"I wasn't gonna say anything, but go with the flow and have fun."

"I am. He's so different from Calvin. He's interested in my passion, and he supports it. He's read all my books, and he even wanted to know about the writing process. And he does the simplest things, but it's still a big deal to me. Like yesterday, we went fishing. And today, he came over, and we sat around vibing to music. It was the most intimate thing I've experienced in a long time," I expressed.

"Dang..." she sighed. "Must be nice."

"Yep, but anyway, how are you?"

"Let's see. I'm tired as hell from working and dealing with this bad ass baby, but other than that I'm making it."

"Aww... You'll have to come down to visit me when I finally get settled."

"I most definitely will." She smiled.

"Choc, where you at?!" EJ hollered. "Come help me get these groceries!"

"Here I come!" I yelled back. "I gotta go, Apryl. I'll call you back later tonight or tomorrow. Love ya."

"Ok. Love you too." She smiled before disconnecting.

***

Late that night, I laid in bed unable to turn my brain off even though I was exhausted. It had nothing to do with writing, but rather my time away from home. *Calvin. What the hell had I been doing with him besides wasting almost a year and a half? If I would've stayed here, Denim and I would've been six years strong. Girl, shut the hell up! Why are you even thinking about this?!* I was doing way too much, so I threw the covers back. Hopefully mama still drank chamomile tea and had a couple of bags somewhere in one of the kitchen cabinets.

After finding a box of sleepy time tea, I microwaved a mug of water, dipped the tea bags in it, and carried it to the couch. I flicked on the lamp and noticed that I'd left my notebook on the coffee table. Greasy fingerprints were visible on the floral cover. EJ's nosy ass had been reading my stuff. I grabbed it and a pen before releasing my thoughts on paper. Soon my eyes became heavy as I paused to sip the last swallow of tea.

***

EJ towered over me in her blue Wal-Mart vest. "What you doing on the couch?"

"I couldn't sleep last night, so I came in here." I attempted to massage the stiffness from my neck. "What time is it?"

"Time for you to wake your ass up!"

"You make me sick!" I rolled my eyes before rising from the couch.

"It's ten minutes to nine."

"Why didn't you wake me up sooner so I could fix you some breakfast?"

"Because I overslept. I gotta get going before I'm late."

"Ok, EJ. Have a good day."

"You too, Miss Sensual." She stopped at the front door. "I'm stopping by Chris's place on my lunch break, so I'll see you when I get off."

"Alright," I replied.

After washing my face and brushing my teeth, I decided to take a nice relaxing bath and then dive into another writing session. The goal was to finish the book and contact someone about designing a cover for it. I ran the water as hot as I could stand it and dumped in some powdered milk. A deep sigh escaped my lips as I sank down in the tub and closed my eyes.

***

I wiped pizza grease from my hands, ending my fifteen minute break, and jumped back into my project. I'd made it to another spicy sex scene. My mind was in a PornHub type space as my fingers rapidly tapped the keys.

He wrapped his hand around her throat, applying slight pressure to her windpipe, as he plunged roughly into her tight vagina. This is what Joanna had craved and fantasized about countless times. "Oh my God! Denim!" she screamed out in pain and pleasure.

Realizing what I'd accidentally typed and how my own temperature was rising, I paused.

"What the hell? It's time to just quit for a while." I quickly corrected the name and closed my computer.

Three light taps sounded at the front door.

"Who is it?" I called.

"It's me!" Denim hollered back.

I hopped up, smoothing my big wild hair and attempting to pull down the bottoms of my lounge set.

As I opened the door, he stood there dressed in what looked like work clothes and holding a large ziplock bag of fish filets.

"Hey!" I smiled.

"Hey!" He studied me closely. "You alright? You look flustered."

"I'm fine. I was sitting here working on my book."

"Oh..."

"You wanna come in?" I stepped aside to allow him entry.

"Naw. I mean, I wish I could stay and chill, but I have to go help Mr. Percy fix some leaks. I'm just stopping by to give you some of this fish that we caught."

"Oh. Well, thank you." I took the bag from his hand. "Tell Mr. Percy I said hello."

I swallowed hard as his eyes raked over my leopard print crop top and matching bottoms.

"I will. See you later, Choc." He turned to descend the steps.

"I'll probably fry some of this up before EJ gets off. You can come over and eat with us. That's if you want to..."

He glanced back, grinning. "I'll definitely be back."

***

"They had the nerve to give me a warning for speaking the truth and shaming the devil. Right is right!" EJ jabbered, stepping into the house with Denim on her heels.

I pulled the last two pieces of fish from the grease as they entered the kitchen. "What is she talking about? What's going on now?"

"I got in trouble for telling a pastor's wife that God isn't pleased with her nasty attitude. She called corporate on me!" EJ squeezed hand soap in one hand and passed it to Denim with the other. "I swear I hate that place. I need a job where I don't have to interact with the public."

They both washed their hands before taking a seat at the dinner table.

"EJ, I told you about your mouth. Sometimes it's best to just zip it," I commented, standing on my toes to grab plates from the cabinet.

"I know, but this time I was doing God's work. He gon' bless me for putting her in her place."

I glanced at Denim, who was laughing, as I shook my head.

"So what you been doing, while you standing up there dressed all hoochafied?" she continued.

My face scrunched. "Hoochafied?"

"Nasty, provocative, like a hoochie! Let me find out..."

"This ain't provocative! And I been writing." I carried over Denim's plate and drink first and then hers.

"Mhmm... What you been doing today, Denim?"

"Been working. Had to fix some leaks," he responded.

I could tell by the expression on her face that she was about to take things to the extreme.

"What was leaking? Choc?" She simpered.

I wanted the wooden floors to open up and swallow me as Denim let out an enormous belly laugh.

Slamming my plate on the table, I plopped down in the chair next to her. "Yo mouth gon' be leaking if you keep playing with me!"

"I'm sorry, Choc. I was just kidding," she apologized.

"Whatever." I picked up my silverware and began eating.

Denim changed the subject. "How far did you get with your book?"

"I finished. Will you test read it for me?"

"Yeah."

"Excuse me, but I'm not illiterate." EJ butted in. "I like to read too."

"But you are always busy."

"You should let him read that poem that you wrote about- Oww!"

I kicked her hard as my phone began to vibrate against the tabletop. "That's mama. Again."

"Hey, ma!" EJ blurted when the call connected. "Choc has been abusing me!"

"Girl...." Mama chuckled. "What are y'all doing?"

"Hey, ma! We're eating dinner with Denim," I answered.

"Oh. Hey, Denim!"

"Hey, Ms. Roz!" He spoke.

"What you doing, ma?" I asked.

"Thinking about my babies."

"Ma, you're supposed to be enjoying your getaway, not worrying about us. We are grown women," EJ stated.

"Yeah, ma. We want you to enjoy yourself. We're fine. Plus we have Denim here if we need anything," I added.

"I'm doing too much, huh? I can take a hint, girls."

"We just want you to relax and not stress so much. What's the point of a vacation if you're gonna constantly worry about home."

"Plus I told you the other day that I got them, Ms. Roz," Denim remarked.

"She called you?" I mouthed.

He nodded.

"What time is it there?" I asked.

"It's a little after seven. Why?"

"It's the perfect time for you to get dressed and go out somewhere with your man, whom I can't wait to meet."

"I can't wait to meet you either!" I heard him say in the background.

"Ok, baby," she chuckled. "I'll talk to you later. Love ya'll."

"Love you too," we all responded simultaneously.

We made small talk and ate the rest of our meal without any more of EJ's shenanigans.

***

"What's going on with you and Denim?" EJ questioned as we washed and dried the dishes.

"Nothing."

"The way y'all look at each other says different. You try to be slick with your peeks, but I notice them. And the way he reacts whenever you speak, hanging onto every word. You still want him, don't you?"

I sighed deeply. "Yes, EJ. I do. Real bad. Do you think I'm a floozy?"

She fell out laughing. "Floozy?! That's something mama would say! But no. Do you think you're one?"

"I just got out of a relationship, and here I am not even a week later having thoughts about someone else."

"Sounds like old feelings coming back to the surface to me, and I'm here for it."

I hung the pot on the rack and put the last plate away. "I need your help with something. He's supposed to go with me to take the car back tomorrow, and then we're going out to eat. I have no idea what to wear. I didn't bring any date-worthy clothes with me."

"He is? Good!" She grabbed my hand, pulling me towards her bedroom. "I gotcha! Come on!"

***

"Quick question, do you wanna put them watermelons on display or nah?" She held up a top with a plunge neckline.

"I don't know."

"Try it on."

My bare breasts bounced as I removed my cami to slip it on.

"Damn! Your titties sit up like that without a bra! I'm so jealous!" EJ exclaimed.

The top was cute, but it'd probably be cool tomorrow night. I didn't want my hardened nipples on display. "This ain't gon' work."

She passed me a mustard yellow long sleeve cropped wrap top. "Alright. What about this?"

"This is cute." I quickly removed the other top.

"Yeah, and you can wear a bra with it. Have them melons sitting up under your chin. It also shows off your flat stomach and your small waist. And it'll pop against your skin."

I tied it and faced the mirror. "I really like this."

"Now that we have a top, let's find some bottoms." She rummaged through her closet and pulled out some high rise dark wash jeans. "Try these."

I slipped off my shorts and jumped to pull them up.

"Walk in them," she instructed.

"What?"

"Walk."

She nodded her approval as I strutted across the room. "Alright now, Miss NBA! Nothing but ass!"

"You are a clown!" I laughed.

"I should become a stylist. We got the top and bottoms. Now we need some shoes." She held her chin as she thought. "Chunky heel or stiletto? That negro might try to be all romantic and roam the city with you, so I'm leaning towards chunky."

I watched her remove some shoe boxes from her closet.

She opened up one that contained a pair of cognac mid-shaft slouch boots.

"Oooh, those!" I sat down on the bed and slipped them on my feet.

She placed her hand on her wide hip. "That does look good. What would you do without me?"

"I don't know. Thanks, EJ!" I grinned.

Chapter 8

"You need to calm the hell down," I whispered to myself.

I could hardly contain myself, and the fact that my book was finished gave me nothing to do today. Deciding to make a grocery store run, I slipped on some shoes and grabbed the car keys from the dresser.

First, I decided to make a quick stop at the hair store for some gold hair accessories and more Mielle pomegranate and honey products. At least that was the plan. I wound up browsing every aisle, tossing head scarves, makeup, lashes, and everything in between into my carrier. After spending a cool hundred bucks, I headed in the direction of Winn-Dixie.

***

I slid my reading glasses onto my face and read the signs in search of pecans and other ingredients that I'd need to make pralines and cookies. Christmas was a little less than a week away, and I wanted to make some sweet treats for EJ and I to enjoy. I also needed to get the ingredients for the gumbo that I planned to make.

"You did not come here for another notebook or pens," I chastised myself as I hurriedly pushed the cart past the office supply aisle.

With the small cart full of goods, I headed to self-checkout.

***

It was about 2:30 when I made it back to the house, giving me plenty of time to get ready. I put my groceries away and headed to the bathroom. I kept my eye on the clock as I bathed. After drying off, I lotioned up and did my skincare routine. Then I started on my hair. I wanted to do a deep part with a couple of cornrows on the side. I added a little razzle dazzle with some gold cuffs. Next, I started on my makeup. I did a nice beat and applied mink lashes before finishing my look off with a coat of Maybelline SuperStay lip color. Dressed and accessorized to perfection, I sprayed on some Killian's Love, Don't Be Shy perfume.

A text from Denim came through right on time.

Denim: You ready to roll?

Me: Yep. Walking out now

Denim was already in his car when I made it outside, so I called him as I hit the locks on the key fob.

"I'm gonna stop at the gas station by the interstate to put a little gas in here, and then we'll hit the slab."

"Alright. I need to gas up anyway," he responded.

I slid into the driver's seat, cranked up, connected my phone, and selected a playlist. A few moments later, I pulled out with Denim trailing behind me.

***

I pulled up to a pump, grabbed some cash out of my bag, and prepared to exit the car when Denim tapped lightly on the window. As I let it down, a cool breeze blew, pulling in the scent of his cologne.

"How much you wanna put in the tank?" he asked.

"Just enough to get me there."

"I'll pay for it and pump it."

I tried to hand him the cash, but he declined it. I let the window back up and watched him walk into the gas station. A group of females, in just as much awe as me, stopped and stared.

Once we fueled up, we hit the interstate. The playlist of tracks from some of Louisiana's local rappers that EJ made had me hype. I bounced in my seat as I accelerated on the highway. Denim's name flashed across my screen, putting a stop to it.

"Hello?" I answered.

"Damn, Choc! You floating!"

"In that car you drive, you should have no issues keeping up."

"I don't, but I'm not tryna get a ticket either."

I eased off the gas a little. "Ok. I'll slow down."

"Alright. I'mma let you go, so you can concentrate on the road."

A call from hot girl Rozlyn came through the second I hung up with Denim.

"Hey, hot girl!" I answered.

"Hey! What are you doing?" she questioned.

"I'm actually on my way to the city to return this rental."

"You and EJ? You girls be careful."

"Actually, EJ is at work."

She gasped. "You're by yourself? It's not safe to be traveling alone, especially down there!"

I blew out. "Ma, you need to calm down! Of course I'm not going by myself. How would I get home? I have Denim following me."

"Ok, and who's gonna be there with EJ?"

"EJ's not gonna be sitting at home by herself. She's going out with her friends when she gets off work." I instantly regretted telling EJ's business.

"What friends?! It's too much going on for her to just be traipsing around in the streets! That girl is going to drive me insane! Hold on! Let me call you right back!"

"No, ma! You stay on the line, and don't call her or text her with all that fussing. She's twenty, and it's a Saturday. Let her go out and have fun."

"Y'all just don't understand! You're young, and you don't think about the wicked things that can happen in the world. I cannot and I do not have the strength to lose another child," she stated in a shaky voice. "I knew I shouldn't have left her down there. She promised me that she'd only go to work and come home. The only reason I felt comfortable leaving her is because Denim would be right across the street, and then you said you were coming."

"Ma, you need to calm down."

"Don't tell me to calm down, Aaliyah!" she yelled.

I took a deep breath, realizing that my mother was having a moment. I understood more than she may have thought I did. I knew that there was this lingering fear of losing another child. After Brandon's death, she kept us on a tight leash. Poor EJ, being the baby, always got it worse than me. The only reason I was able to escape to California is because I snuck and transferred. Using some of my share of the insurance money, I'd already covered everything that financial aid wouldn't. We had this big blowup about which one of us knew what was best for me. Even though she'd been beyond pissed at first, she realized that I wasn't going to let her control me in that situation. The decision for me to complete the second semester of my junior year and the rest of my studies in another state had already been made. I think in a lot of ways it proved my independence. Now it was time for her to loosen the reins on EJ.

"Ma, Brandon is dead. And I'm so sorry you have to deal with that hurt, but EJ is not. Let her live."

She cried softly on the other end.

"You pray for us, don't you?"

"Every single day." She sniffled.

"Well, we're covered. We've always been covered. Even Brandon, he was covered. You wanna know how I had to learn to see it?" I put on my signal and switched lanes.

"How, Choc?"

"What happened to him, the things that they did, wasn't of God. But because Brandon was covered, he found comfort in His arms. I know the human side of you worries, but you have no control over death. You just have to trust God. We shouldn't stop living because one life ended. And I don't think Bran would want us to."

"Ok, baby."

"I want you to go get yourself together, and I will tell EJ to call you before she leaves and when she makes it back. And I will call you when I make it back to the house. Alright?"

"Alright, sweetie. I love you, and I'm sorry."

"I love you more, and you don't have to be sorry. I'll talk to you later."

"Whew!" I breathed once the call ended. "That lady almost made me mess up my makeup."

***

Having returned my rental, I slid into the passenger seat of Denim's ride. The intoxicating scent of his cologne filled the interior and my nostrils.

"You smell good!" we said at the same time.

"You can smell my perfume? I don't smell nothing but you." I chuckled.

He smiled. "Yes ma'am, and you look good too. I like what you did to your hair."

"Thank you. You don't look too bad yourself." I eyed him as he navigated the car out of the parking lot and onto the busy street.

He was dressed in a simple black tee, black distressed jeans, an olive green jacket, and brown boots. The only jewelry he wore were the diamond studs in his ears and a gold watch. Not wanting to come off as creepy, I shifted my focus to the city's buildings. It was like being in one of those holiday movies. The only thing missing was snow. The buildings, palm trees, and streetcars were decorated with lights and bows. Pretty soon, we were pulling into the parking lot of a small restaurant.

"I heard some good stuff about this lil spot, so I thought we'd see what they working with," Denim stated.

"Sounds good to me." I couldn't wait to see what they had to offer either.

***

"It's nice in here," I commented as we took our seats.

He nodded in agreement. "Yeah, it is."

The place had a homey cozy feel to it with framed southern artwork on the walls. It was also decorated with garland and holiday knick knacks, and a large Christmas tree was set up in one corner.

The more I read the menu, the more difficult it became to choose what I wanted to eat.

"You got any idea of what you wanna get?" I asked. "My greedy ass wants some of everything."

"Me too. This place will make you hurt yourself." He continued to turn the menu's pages. "They have an ultimate platter. It says it's enough for two to share. You wanna try that?"

"Sure. And I think for my drink I want to try their Jingle Juice."

"Where you see that at?"

I pointed to the cover of the holiday drink menu. He grabbed it and read the ingredients.

"Now, Choc, I don't know about that. You used to get drunk off two wine coolers, and this has a lot of alcohol in it. Plus I wanna take you somewhere else after we leave here."

"I grew out of that." I chuckled. "But since you got other plans for me, I'll go with a sweet tea."

***

"This food good as hell!" Denim exclaimed, popping another crispy fried oyster into his mouth.

I reached for another alligator bite. "Mhmm." I speared the last one with my fork. "Here."

He leaned forward and parted his full lips. Our eyes met, and butterflies began to flutter in my belly.

The waitress returned to check on us, interrupting the moment. "Are you guys ok? You need anything?"

"Actually, I'd like to get a slice of Cajun cake," I replied.

"You got room for cake?" Denim's nose scrunched. "I'm stuffed."

"Yes! I am in heaven. They didn't have this kind of stuff in Cali. I mean, they have Cajun restaurants, but they ain't hittin' like the ones here."

"What was your life like over there?"

Unlike the first time he'd asked, I was willing to open up a little bit.

"When I first got there, I felt out of place, like a country bumpkin. Everybody carried themselves differently from me, and I had this southern accent and spoke incorrect English. I wasn't sociable at all. I'd go to class, and therapy, and then back to my apartment until I got a part-time job at a bookstore/coffee shop. I spent all my free time reading and writing. That's how my first book came about."

"How did you get to the point of publishing it?" He placed his elbows on the table and leaned in a little closer.

"Apryl. She was the only friend I made, and that's because she wouldn't leave me alone, even though I didn't talk much. She read it and convinced me to self-publish it on Amazon. I did, and we promoted the hell out of it on social media. It eventually became a success." I sat back in my seat as the waitress placed the slice of cake in front of me. "Then I signed to a publisher and started making just as much as I would at a full time job. That's when I realized that I could make a career out of it. "

"I'm very proud of you, Choc. What you've been through, the way you started over by yourself, your success with your writing. Not many people can do that."

"Yeah, well it all eventually went to shit." I put a piece of the cake into my mouth.

He frowned. "Don't think like that. Some aspects may not have gone the way you thought they would, but that doesn't take away from the good."

"I guess you're right. It did lead me back home, and I feel a sense of peace that was missing when I was away." *And I get to be around you.* I thought.

***

This was my first time experiencing Celebration in the Oaks, but it definitely wouldn't be my last. My fingers intertwined with Denim's as we strolled the park. There were a plethora of lights and Christmas displays.

"If this doesn't get you in the holiday spirit, nothing will," I commented.

"Christmas usually ain't a big deal to me, but it's a little better this year."

"How do you usually spend Christmas?" I asked.

"I usually go to my mama's. She remarried and stays in Mississippi now," he replied.

"You have to tell Ms. Dana I said hello."

"I will, but I'll take you to see her soon. Now how did you usually spend Christmas? I'm pretty sure the rich do it big for the holidays."

"Actually, they don't. I guess because they can afford whatever all year round they don't have to show out like us average folks. To answer your question, I would go with Calvin to his mother's, and we'd eat a big breakfast and exchange gifts. Then we'd return home and Calvin would go to work."

"So you spent the majority of your day alone?"

"Yep. I wasn't really in the holiday spirit then anyway." I stopped in front of a snowman display. "Denim, what would be the ultimate Christmas gift for you?"

"Choc, I don't want you to get me nothing."

"There's gotta be something you want but haven't gotten yet."

"Listen to me good." He placed a finger underneath my chin. "I don't want you going out and buying me nothing."

"Why? This holiday season is extra special to me, and I wanna get you a gift."

"It can still be special without you getting me anything. Plus I don't think money can buy what I want."

"Ok..." I relented.

***

"Yea! Don't stop jiggin!" Denim sang and bobbed his head to the track that floated from his speakers. "Aye! Get it, Choc!"

I had no idea what I was doing, but I was turnt. Plus we'd stopped and gotten a daiquiri. The kick was just as strong as the sweetness, so I was a little tipsy.

"You lit as fuck!" He laughed.

The music changed to "Gotta Move On (Queen's Remix)" but the vibe didn't.

"This my shit!" I hollered. "Turn it up a little bit more!"

I rapped along, clapped, and did a lil Harlem shake. "Come on, Denim! Dance with me!"

Always down for my goofy shenanigans, he joined in. Our car karaoke lasted until he pulled into my driveway.

"I had a really good time with you tonight, Denny," I said softly, my eyes on his. "I haven't had this much fun in a long time."

"I made it back to being called Denny, huh?" He grinned. "I had a good time too. We'll do it again soon."

"I look forward to it."

He leaned over the center console and cupped my chin. My eyes closed in anticipation of his lips on mine. I was crushed when they landed on my cheek, at the left corner of my mouth.

"Good night, Choc."

I reached for the door handle. "Good night."

**

You are so fucking dumb! He never said it was a date. He no longer looks at you in that way. I twisted the knob on the front door. *EJ's here. At least I have somebody to vent to.*

I was not prepared for the sight before me when I stepped inside.

"Oh my God! Choc!" EJ gasped as she pushed Chris' head from in between her legs.

"EJ, what the fuck?!"

"I'm sorry! I didn't know you were outside!"

"It doesn't matter! Why are you doing that in here instead of in your room?!" I bellowed.

"I'm sorry, Choc. It's not EJ's fault," Chris interjected.

I cut my eyes at him, and he zipped his lips.

Shaking my head, I stormed to my room and slammed the door. I didn't come out until I heard EJ and Chris leave.

After changing into my pajamas, I crossed the hall into the bathroom to wash away my makeup. Then I headed into the kitchen for a cup of hot tea.

EJ re-entered the house and made her way to the kitchen table. "I'm sorry, Choc. I wasn't thinking."

"Whatever," I mumbled.

"I know you ain't that upset about me getting a lil head. What's the matter?"

"Nothing," I lied.

"Yes, it is. What happened on your date?"

"Nothing. Absolutely nothing!"

Her face scrunched. "What?"

"We went out to eat, we went to City Park, we vibed on the way home. It was just like it used to be until we made it here," I explained. "He kissed me on the fucking cheek!"

She burst out laughing. "You mad because of that? This was y'all's first time going out in a long time. You wanted him to tongue you down like they do in the movies?"

My head hung. "Yes."

"You know what your problem is?" She didn't give me a chance to respond. "Your feelings for him never changed, so you expect things to just be the same. It doesn't work like that, sista girl. You're the one that left. The ball is in his court now. You're on his time, not yours."

"You're right."

"I'm always right."

"If you say so. Now get in there and clean that loveseat with your nasty ass. I should tell mama on you."

She grabbed some paper towels and disinfectant. "Please don't!"

Chapter 9

"Good morning, Miss Sensual!" EJ grinned as I passed through the living room to get to the kitchen.

"Good morning, Shawnna!"

"Shawnna?"

"I was getting some head, getting getting some head," I sang, noticing her attire and slowing my stride. "That doesn't look like work clothes to me."

"Shut up!" She laughed. "And I'm not going to work today. You need to go get dressed because we're having a girls day."

"This early?"

"It's not that early. Plus we gon' take a ride to Baton Rouge, get breakfast, and do some other stuff."

I spun on my heels. "Let me go change then."

***

"What's wrong with you?" EJ asked ten minutes into the ride.

"Nothing."

"Yes, it is. You being way too quiet. You still overthinking that Denim situation?"

"No." I shifted a bit in the leather seat. "EJ, were you ever mad at me for leaving?"

"Choc, why are you asking me this now, almost three years later?"

"Because we never talked about it, and I wanna know."

"No, I was not mad. Sad, yes. I understood you leaving, but I didn't understand you not coming back at all."

Guilt began to eat me up.

She glanced at me out of the corner of her eye. "Uh-uh! No crying in here!"

"I'm sorry. I thought that if I came back, I'd be this heaping weeping mess. I just knew that I wouldn't be able to function. And every time I invited ya'll to Cali, y'all couldn't come, so I stopped asking."

"It was a different struggle here without Brandon's income. You know he took care of a large portion of the bills. I was trying to work part-time and go to school while mama got a second job."

"How come y'all never told me y'all were struggling that bad? I would've sent more money?"

"We didn't want to worry you. And what were you gonna do, start funneling the doctor's money?"

"I would've had my entire royalty checks deposited into mama's account," I answered.

"No, Choc, that's your money that you worked hard for. And we're good now thanks to Andrew. He owns a trucking company, so..." She rubbed her fingers together, indicating money. "And he's so nice. I like him for mama. He brings out a happier side of her. I know you'll like him."

"I'm sure I will."

"Can I ask you something? It's about your second day here."

"Go ahead." I dug around my purse in search of my pack of Trident.

"Why were you dodging Denim?"

I removed a piece of gum and handed her one. "Because I hurt his feelings when I left, and we stopped talking. I thought he was still holding onto that."

"It's so interesting seeing you and him interact these days."

"Why you say that?"

"Because you packed that love and took it with you, and then you returned with it almost three years later. Did you really love Calvin, or were you just settling because of what you assumed about Denim?"

"Calvin was charming and fun, at first. We had a great connection, and when I was with him, I didn't feel as sad. So, yes, I did love him. Not the way that I loved Denim though. I thought about Denim almost every day."

"You thought about Denim that much, but you were engaged to another man. You don't see the problem here?" She side eyed me as she slowed down for the traffic light.

It seemed as if she had more sense than me these days.

She shook her head. "Young, dumb, wasting time, and getting full of an older man's cum."

"I wasn't getting full of much of anything these last few months," I scoffed.

"You and the doctor need help. He wasn't your first choice, and he expected to keep a young woman without giving her dick on the regular. Tuh! Two fools!"

"Ok, Eleisha! I get it." I huffed. "I didn't make the best decisions, but I'm learning from them. I don't wanna talk about this anymore."

"I bet you don't." She changed the song that was playing and turned up the volume.

***

"Why would you wait until right before Christmas to do your shopping?" So far, we'd gone to four stores.

"Everybody doesn't start shopping two months ahead of time like you do. Plus I only have a couple more things to get. Let's go in here." She pointed at a menswear store. "They might have something I can get for Chris."

I stood off to the side as she browsed their racks.

"Did you get Denim a gift?"

"No," I replied. "He said Christmas would still be special without exchanging gifts."

"He said Christmas would still be special without exchanging gifts!" she mocked. "Look at your chipmunk cheeks all red."

"Shut up!"

"You like this shirt?" She held up a flannel button down.

"Yeah. I'd wear that myself. Oversized with a black crop top, tights, and some boots. Do they have it in a medium?"

"This is a medium." She passed it to me. "I think I might need to get Chris a size small. He so damn boney."

I walked away as she reached into her purse for her vibrating phone. Grabbing my own, I shot Denim a text.

Me: Hey! What you doing?

He hit me back within seconds.

Denim: I was just thinking about you, but I'm bout to ride out to Mr. Percy's to get his truck and wash it. You wanna come?

Me: Actually, I'm out and about with Looney Toon.

Denim: EJ *laughing face emoji* Tell her I said hey

Me: I will.

Denim: Y'all wanna come over to eat and chill with me later?

Me: Hell yeah! Just let me know what time

Denim: Ok

EJ crept up behind me. "Mmm... let me find out!"

"I was talking to Denim."

"I already know that."

"He invited us to eat and chill at his house later. You wanna go?"

Her eyes lit up. "Yeah. Girl, his shit is laid! I went over there one time to bring him something and didn't want to leave. You'll see."

"Ok, EJ." I chuckled.

"Anyway, that was mama calling me. She was acting weird."

"How?"

"She was calm, and she didn't ask me a million and ten questions. She usually wants to know where I'm at, who I'm with, what color underwear I have on, if I'm wearing a panty-liner..."

"You so doggone silly!" I cackled.

"But you get what I'm saying." She twittered.

"Yeah, I do. She's trying to do better with you."

"You must've said something to her, or Jesus is about to come down from the clouds."

"We may have had a talk." I smiled.

***

EJ had been right about Denim's house. It was an older model, but the inside had been completely renovated. The living room walls were painted a cool blue with white trim and a large sectional set in the center of the room framing a glass coffee table. A large smart TV was mounted on the wall between a built-in that held some candles, framed photos of him, Brandon, and the rest of his family, and a few knickknacks. Recessed lighting illuminated the space. The floor plan was open, so there was little to no separation between the living room, dining room, and kitchen. A large island sat in the middle of the kitchen that held white cabinets and updated stainless steel appliances.

"This is nice," I complimented.

"Told you," she whispered.

"Courtesy of my mama and her decorating skills, but thank you." Denim grinned. "I figured we could eat and watch a movie."

"Ok." I nodded.

"It smells good. What you got over there?" EJ inched closer to the kitchen.

"Fried chicken, greens, and cornbread."

"You cooked all that?" I asked.

"Greens and cornbread compliments of Mr. Percy. Fried chicken catered by Popeyes. Y'all can go ahead and fix a plate. I got a couple beers, cold dranks, and water in the fridge," he stated.

We walked into the kitchen and grabbed one of the saucers along with utensils that he'd sat out before fixing our plates.

"EJ!" I scolded as she dished up a large portion of greens.

"What?!"

"You ain't at home! Greedy ass!"

"It's cool." Denim laughed. "Get what you want, EJ."

"Thank you." She blew a raspberry. "She still tries to act like she's somebody's mama."

"I see."

"Look, now, don't be ganging up on me." I chuckled.

We grabbed some drinks and headed to the couch. Denim being Denim and EJ being EJ, outvoted me and chose some horror film instead of the holiday movie that I wanted to watch.

Mr. Percy put his foot in them greens, and I wound up going back for seconds. Full and relaxed, I laid my head back on the couch, closed my eyes, and let the itis have its way with me.

Suddenly, a guttural scream blasted from the surround sound, nearly giving me a heart attack. Clutching my chest, Fred Sanford style, I jumped out of my sleep and farted loud and hard.

"Got 'em!" EJ and Denim hollered in laughter.

She could barely catch her breath. "Denim, where is your bathroom?!" She snorted. "I'm bout to pee on myself!"

He clutched his abdomen. "It's down the hall, second door on the right."

"Y'all make me sick!" I tooted my lips. "I should've known."

Those two used to constantly prank me.

"We had to do it for old time's sake." Denim continued to laugh. "I wasn't expecting you to fart like that though."

"You got that one, but revenge is sweet."

EJ returned to the couch. "Man, I haven't laughed like that in a minute. Them drawers probably got a hole in them. Denim, you better check your couch when we leave."

I playfully rolled my eyes. "Alright now, Eleisha!"

I got back comfortable as Denim unpaused the movie and draped his arm over my shoulder.

***

"Thank you for inviting us over." We stood on Denim's steps. "I had fun with you clowns."

"No. Thank y'all for keeping me company. We gotta do this again soon." He smiled.

"Most definitely." EJ yawned loudly.

He pulled us in for a group hug. "Good night."

"Good night," we replied in unison.

"I'll hit you up tomorrow, Choc." He placed a kiss on my forehead.

Chapter 10

"Hey, Apryl! I was gonna call you last night, but I got in kind of late." I shifted my phone over to my left ear and shoulder. "I'm about to go check out the library and try to start a new book."

"You really going hard, huh?"

I made my way towards my mom's room in search of her car keys. "Yeah. You know I used to drop something every other month. Anyway, what are you doing?"

"Just sitting around relaxing. My mom came and got the baby," she replied. "I wish you were here. You know I don't really associate with anyone else."

"I miss you too." I picked up one of the framed family portraits that sat on the bureau.

We'd taken that pic about a year before Brandon's death.

I miss you, Bran. I thought as I put it back in its place.

I opened the top drawer and grabbed the keys. As I turned to leave, I glimpsed a silhouette moving towards his old room.

"Oh my God!"

"What's the matter?!" Apryl responded hysterically.

"I saw something."

"Saw what?!"

"A shadow. It went towards my brother's old room."

"Aww, girl! You had me worried!" She breathed a sigh of relief. "It's probably just him."

"I know, but I'm not used to seeing that." I closed the bedroom door behind me and went back into the living room to grab my laptop and head out.

"I think it's sweet that he's there watching over you. How have you been feeling since you've been back at home?"

"Actually, it's nothing like I expected it to be. I've only cried once, but I've been happy since then." I smiled.

"That's good. I'm loving this progress that you're making."

Old school music blasted from the speakers as I started the car.

"Well, I'm gonna let you go. Call me when you get back because I want a full report on how things are going with your muse."

"Ok. I will." I chuckled. "Love you."

"Love you too," she remarked.

I browsed the library's larger updated section of African American fiction, spotting all of my books. I felt a sense of pride as I reminisced about how I would spend hours in the library reading others' books. Now I was the one creating some of them. I snapped a few pics to post to my pages before making my way to one of the large window seats.

Once comfortable, I removed my laptop from its case and got to work. I usually listened to music while writing, but there was something soothing about the silence and the overcast outside. My mind wandered to a place far outside the confines of the building and my small town as I typed the start of a ratchet tale.

I was 4K in when my phone began to vibrate. Seeing that it was Denim, I quickly slid the icon to answer it.

"Hello?" I whispered.

"Hey, Chocolate! Why you whispering?"

"I'm at the library."

"How long you plan to be over there?"

"I'm writing, so probably for a while. Why?"

"It's nothing major. I'mma let you get back to it."

"Ok..." I responded, knowing that I'd drop everything in a heartbeat if he wanted to link up. "Talk to you later."

***

I could sense his presence the minute he entered the building. My heart thumped like a bass drum, while heat radiated from my cheeks to the tips of my ears.

"Hi! Welcome to the library!" one of the librarians behind the desk greeted him.

"Hey!" Denim responded politely before acknowledging the other one. "What's up, Natalia?"

"Denim," she sniped.

"Chocolate!" he whispered when he made it over to me.

"Hey, Denny!" I grinned. "What you doing over here?"

He shrugged. "Felt like going to the library."

He sat beside me, picked up one of the books I planned on checking out later, and read the synopsis before placing it back down. "You know what I wanna read?"

"What's that?"

"That book that you just wrote, the one you never sent me."

"Oh, yeah! I'm sorry. I forgot. What's your email address? I'll send it now."

He rattled it off, and I sent a pdf copy.

"Thank you!" He opened it and began reading.

"Ain't you supposed to be typing?" He'd glanced up and caught me staring.

"I am."

"How, if you watching me read?"

"Is it ok? Does it flow?" I quizzed.

"I'll let you know when I finish."

Unable to focus, I closed Google Docs and opened up Facebook. As I scrolled and read the latest gossip, the smell of freshly brewed hazelnut coffee hit my nose. I peeked up as Denim rose to his feet and headed to the coffee maker. He poured some in the small cup, adding extra sugar and even more creamer, and brought it over to me.

"I thought you were fixing some for yourself." The corners of my mouth twitched as I attempted to restrain a smile.

"You got jokes, huh?"

Brandon, EJ, Denim, and I had taken a weekend trip to Orlando one summer. On the way there, I'd convinced Denim to try a cup of coffee. It messed his stomach up so bad that he sharted.

"There better not be no shit on my seats!" I fell into a fit of giggles. "Bran was pissed."

"Nigga swore I'd messed up the seats of his new ride." Denim laughed. *"Choc, go help him clean his ass!"*

Forgetting where we were, I howled. "Oops!" My hand sprang to my lips.

"Sorry," I mouthed to the librarian that stood at the coffee station.

"It's ok." She smiled. "No one else is here."

"Man, we had some fun that weekend."

"Yeah, we did. I miss my brother." I sighed.

"I do too."

The other girl made her way to the coffee station and shot daggers at us.

My top lip curled. "I guess that's Natalia."

His eyes cut in her direction. "Mhmm..."

"What's her problem?"

"She's just somebody that I used to know."

"Oh..." It wasn't hard to read between the lines.

Not giving a damn about her, he continued, "Anyway, we should go on another vacation, make some more memories."

"That would be nice considering that I haven't been on one since then. Maybe we can bring EJ and Chris."

He grinned. "Alright. We'll make something shake when the summer hits."

Natalia inched closer to where we sat, pretending to straighten some books.

"Natalia, will you go outside and check the dropbox?" the other librarian called.

She cast us one last look before ambling away.

"Go ahead and ask, Choc. I know you want to."

"What? All I wanna ask is if you want to see if that wing spot is hitting or missing today."

"Yeah, right." He smirked. "I know you like a book."

"Alright. What happened between you and her? How long ago was it?" I pattered.

His nose and forehead crinkled as he thought about it. "Like five months ago. A whole lot happened, and a whole bunch of nothing happened at the same time. She wanted more than I did. I didn't want to string her along, so I called it quits."

"Umph. At least you didn't feed her lies."

"Damn, your tone..."

"Just thinking about my own experience. He kept making promises that he couldn't keep. Everything came to a head one night, and the next day I packed my bags and dipped."

"Now you here looking at my ugly ass," he joked.

"Yep," I chortled.

"Seriously though, Chocolate, it's his loss." He stood up and reached for my hand. "Let's go get something to eat."

**

"Before we go in, are any of your girlfriends employed here?" I lifted a brow as Denim held open the door to the wing spot.

Hunching a shoulder, he quipped, "I hope so. Maybe I can get us some free food."

We entered the small building that had been converted into a restaurant and found a seat at one of the small metal tables.

The place had a very rustic feel with old paintings and a map of the city adorning the walls. Despite this being an eatery, another odor lingered. It wasn't unpleasant, but you could tell that these doors had been closed for decades.

I scanned the menu. "What good wing flavors have you had from here?"

"I usually get honey hot. Lemon pepper is pretty good too."

"I think I'll get a combination of both and a coke. Oooh, they have fried pickles too!"

He made a face. "You had that before? Fried pickles."

"Nope, but we gonna try them today."

"We?"

"Yes, we. Here comes the waitress."

"Good afternoon! I'm Stacie! What can I get for y'all today?" She grinned.

"I'll have the eight piece traditional wings, half lemon pepper, half honey hot, all flats with an order of fried pickles and a Coke," I replied.

"Ok, and for you, sir? Same ticket or separate?"

"Same!" I blurted. "My treat."

"I'll have the eight piece honey hot traditional wings and a Corona," Denim answered.

She scribbled on her ticket book. "Alrighty. Your food will be out in about ten minutes, but I'll be right back with your drinks."

"I don't want you paying for this," he said the second she walked away .

"Too bad because I am. You can get the bill next time we go out."

"Who said anything about us going out again?"

My hands that rested on the tabletop became my focal point.

He chuckled. "Relax, Choc. I'm just playing."

A wide grin broke across my face.

"I wanna take you out again after Christmas if that's cool with you."

You can do whatever you wanna do with me. I thought but responded, "That's cool."

I grabbed my drink from the waitress, taking a long sip.

"So what's been going on up top?" He tapped his temple. "You been feeling alright?"

Been driving myself insane thinking about you all day and night. "I've been doing fine. Way better than I initially thought I would be. I should've come back a long time ago, but my overthinking..."

"They say the worst place to be is in your own head."

"Yep. I need to work on that. That's my New Year's resolution, to quit thinking the worst and to get in a gym."

His face scrunched. "Get in the gym for what?"

"Because Imma be a mess if I keep eating like I've been doing. I need to at least stay toned."

"Oh, 'cause I was about to say. You don't need to lose a pound. If you ask me, you look good enough to eat."

His words caused my ears and cheeks to heat like a furnace.

My phone started buzzing inside my mini backpack purse. Pulling it out and seeing that it was my mother, I shot her a text and quickly slipped it back into my bag.

"You got a New Year's resolution in mind?" I asked, trying to shift the mood.

He stared at me intensely. "Not necessarily a New Year's resolution since I'm trying to start doing it now, but to love the people that are in my life a little harder."

"That's a good one."

A whiff of the crispy chicken and different sauces hit my nostrils as the waitress strolled over with our food.

"Man, that was fast. I thought she said ten minutes," Denim commented.

I wasted no time picking up one of the wings and going to work. "Mmm... this is so good. They are a hit today."

"Choc, don't do that."

"Do what?"

"*Mmm!*" he mocked. "All that moaning and shit."

"I'm sorry." I tittered. "I have a habit of doing that. It gets on your nerves?"

He took a swig of his beer. "Yes and no. I'm sure you know what I mean."

"Damn pervert. I forgot how your mind stays in the gutter."

"With that shit you be writing, you shouldn't be saying nothing." He laughed. "Ain't no telling what's in that notebook that you so secretive about."

Shrugging a shoulder, I retorted, "Welp, that ruined any chance you ever had of reading anything in it."

"Damn!"

I popped one of the slices of fried pickles into my mouth. "These are good. You gotta try one."

"Naw. I'll pass."

"Denny, you ain't no fun!" I jutted my bottom lip.

"Man, give me one then!"

He made the ugliest face as he chewed and swallowed while I hollered.

"It's not that bad."

"Well, I don't like it." He shuddered. "I don't know why I'm always quick to do whatever you say. The shit costs me everytime."

"Now you're telling lies! You act like I asked you to do something dangerous."

"Yeah, you didn't this time." He cut his eyes at me.

"What are you talking about?

"So you don't remember that summer when you got me stung by bees?!"

I started to choke on my Coke.

"Them flowers on that bush are so pretty! Denny, will you get me some? And what did my dumb ass do? Reached up there and got tore up while you stood there screaming at the top of your lungs." He shook his head. "Love will make you do some dumb shit. Not only did I get clowned by my boys, but I went home and my mama called me a dumb ass."

"But I doctored on you, and some more stuff," I reminded him.

"Yeah, you did."

"Those were some good times."

His eyes rolled slightly. "Yeah, for you." He pushed back from the table. "I have to go to the restroom."

As I nibbled on a pickle and waited for Denim to come back, someone approached our table. "Aaliyah, I thought that was you!"

Who the hell is this? I squinted.

"It's me, David!" He put an extra large set of veneers on display, and his eyes were no longer crossed.

David glowed up, kinda.

I smiled politely. "Oh! Hey, David! I remember you!"

"How you been?" Uninvited, he plopped down in Denim's seat. "Last I heard, you'd moved out west."

"I've been ok, and yes, I did."

He ogled me. "You damn sholl look good!"

"Thanks."

"I was wondering if I could get your number and maybe take you out and catch up."

My eyes traveled across the room to Denim, who'd finally emerged. My answer to David's question only required a simple yes or no, but in true Choc fashion, I had to make things complicated.

"I-uh...I'm his...I'm his...uh..." I stumbled over my words as Denim made it closer to the table.

He stopped behind David. "Excuse me, dawg. You in my seat."

"Oh! What's up, Denim? My bad; I didn't know, man," David apologized before getting up. "It was good seeing you, Aaliyah. Take care."

"You too," I muttered.

Denim top lip curled. "Can't even leave you alone for a few seconds. Got Steve Harvey over here trying to push up on you."

"Demin, you wrong for that!" I shrieked. "And I don't want him. He's liable to be outside starting a rumor about me right this second. You ready to go?" I watched his eyes wander to the bill that sat on the table, so I quickly snatched it up.

***

"You got any plans for Christmas Eve?" he asked as we exited the building.

I replied while struggling to get the car keys out of the small compartment in the front of my bag, "No. EJ's going to a party, so I'll be at home by myself."

"I was wondering if you wanted to spend the evening with me since I'll be gone for Christmas."

"Yes, sir. I do." I peered up at him with a smile on my face.

He opened the car door for me. "Alright." Leaning forward, he pressed his lips to my forehead. "I'm about to go run a few errands. I'll call you later."

"Ok, Denny. Talk to you later." I slid into the driver's seat, got situated, and prepared to close the door.

"Oh yeah, Choc!" He called. "What were you going to say in there? You're my what?"

I shrugged. "Whatever you want me to be, Denim."

He displayed a Cheshire Cat grin as I shut the door and crank up the car.

***

"Wow! You put yourself out there like that?!" Apryl gasped as I shared the rundown on my day. "That's how you feel within a week?"

"Well, I wasn't gonna lie to him. And yes, today made a week that I've been back, but it's deeper than just being infatuated after running into an old fling."

"You're gonna have to explain that to me, ma'am. All you've shared is that he's an old friend that lives next door."

I let out a dreamy sigh. "Denim and my brother were best friends since like second grade, so he'd always been around. He was more like a brother to me until I hit puberty and started having these thoughts about him. But he wasn't worried about my nerdy ass back then. Years later, something changed, and Denim became my first everything."

"That's a beautiful story, kinda like something out of a book," she stated.

"But it's not out of a book. Every day I'm craving that old thing and wishing I could turn back the hands of time. Don't get me wrong. I'm getting a small taste of it, but I want it all."

"You wanna be his woman."

"Mmhmm, and you know what, Apryl?" I sipped from my glass of red wine. "As much as I used to want things to work out between me and Calvin, I'm glad they didn't."

"Speaking of, we have a cold red," she whispered, letting me know that he'd entered the break room. "I'll text you on my next break."

"Talk to you later," I responded before hitting the end button.

I got up to connect my phone to the charger when everything went pitch black.

"What the hell?" I mumbled. "The power would go out when I'm here by myself."

Being the scaredy cat that I was, I climbed into the bed and pulled the top cover over my head.

"Chocolate!" Denim called from the porch.

Thank God! I threw the comforter back, slipped my feet into my house shoes, and used my phone's flashlight to guide me to the door.

When I opened it, he stood there holding a large flashlight. "Come take a walk with me."

"A walk? Are you crazy?!" I side eyed him. "You're more than welcome to come inside and sit with me until the power comes back on, but a walk is out of the question. It's pitch black out there."

"I have a flashlight, and we won't go far. Just come with me for a minute."

"No! There might be wild dogs or something running around."

His laughter pierced the night's stillness. "Girl, ain't no wild dogs out here. I'm not gonna let nothing get you. I just wanna show you something right quick. Come on."

Sighing deeply, I stepped onto the porch and closed the door behind me.

***

My head swiveled in every direction at any and every little sound.

Denim chuckled. "You need to relax before you trip over your own feet. We almost there."

As we cut through one of the neighbor's yards, I knew exactly where we were going.

"I know you not bringing me to the field!" I whispered.

"Yeah, but not for that." He held my hand, leading me through the narrow pathway before coming upon the clearing.

The field was a couple of acres of land that held a small pond. This was once our spot to engage in freaky business whenever we couldn't afford a hotel room. This was also the place where we'd made future plans to get married after I graduated college and to have two kids, a boy and a girl.

Tonight the atmosphere was different. The full moon and the stars seemed more noticeable, closer to the earth, now that they were the main source of light.

"I've never taken notice of the sky like this before. It's beautiful," I commented as we stopped and had a seat in the lush grass.

"I have. This is my spot where I come to clear my head and pray. I think about you a lot too when I'm here."

I leaned over and rested my head on his shoulder. "Denny, how come you never tried to reach out to me?"

He sighed. "The timing wasn't right. Just like you was dealing with shit, so was I. The only person I needed to be reaching out to was God."

"Oh..."

"I was going through a lot, having vile thoughts. I was so angry. Many days, I thought about going down there and taking one of their people just so they could feel the same type of pain. That ain't like me, so I had to pray that wickedness away." I could hear the pain in his voice as he shared his darkest moments.

"I'm so sorry. I feel like an inconsiderate bitch. I never thought about how things might've been for anybody else." A tear slid down my cheek. "I was so focused on myself."

"Choc, don't cry. You did what you were supposed to do, and that's focusing on your own healing. I did want to reach out to you when I felt I'd gotten past most of my turmoil, but you'd moved on by then. It wouldn't have been right for me to try to insert myself back into your life, so I tried to move on too. That was a damn disaster every single time. I ain't affectionate enough, and I don't know how to open up. That's what they said."

I caressed his back. "That ain't the person that I know."

"Of course, it ain't." He chuckled. "I didn't come out here for this, and you got me laying all my stuff bare. We supposed to be stargazing."

"Let's focus on the stars then." Something brushed against my leg. "Ahh! What the fuck is that?!" I shrieked.

"Girl..." He chortled. "Relax, that's just my hand."

"Ok, but I still hear something over there." I gestured towards the bushes that lined the field.

"That's just a herd of deer. Come sit in between my legs if you're that scared."

Getting that close to that part of his body was one thing that I did not need to do, or I'd really go insane.

"I'm good." My face contorted as he laughed softly. "What's so funny?"

"You." He switched positions and stretched out flat on his back, extending an arm. "Lay back and put your head right here."

We sprawled out in the middle of the field, just breathing and admiring God's work.

If what we get to see is this beautiful, I can't imagine what heaven and the things unknown are like. But Brandon gets to experience it. I thought.

"Choc, you good?" Denim whispered.

"Just thinking about my brother."

"You wanna leave? We can go back to my house."

"No. We don't have to leave. I'm ok." I shifted until my head was on his chest.

His phone dinged in his side pocket. He reached for it and read the message. "The lights are back on."

Neither one of us made a move to get up.

***

"Excuse me, young lady! Where have you been?" EJ fussed as I entered the house.

I yawned loudly. "Outside with Denim. Your hair is pretty."

She'd gotten it braided when she got off work.

"Thank you, but let me find out."

"Whatever. I'm going to bed. Good night. Love you." I made my way towards the hallway.

"Mhmm... Love you too. And you came back tired."

"EJ, please." I laughed.

Chapter 11

"What the hell?" I muttered as I passed by EJ.

The crazy girl was sitting up in the arm chair asleep, looking like a propped up corpse. I made my way to the refrigerator, grabbed my bottle of Smartwater with the flip up top, and tip toed back into the living room. Putting it close to her face, I squeezed. She gasped and flailed around like she was in the deep end of a pool.

"Wake your ass up!" I hollered.

"Choc, why would you do that?!" She hopped up, mean mugging me.

"The same reason why y'all decided to scare me the other day. Now get up, and brush your teeth. I'm about to make us some breakfast."

***

"EJ, why you not talking to me? You really that mad over a prank?" I added sugar and a lot of evaporated milk to my oatmeal.

"Hell yeah! I already didn't sleep well, and here you come with that mess. Then I went to the bathroom and saw that my period came. Now I can't even get none for Christmas," she grouched.

"I'm sorry, but three of those things have nothing to do with me. And why in the world were you sitting up in that chair anyway?"

"My head was too sore to lay down in my bed."

"My Lord." I shot her a sympathetic look.

"And they better not come messing with me at work today 'cause I'm liable to go off," she ranted.

"You need to chill out. Your day hasn't even started yet." Pushing back from the table, I headed to the medicine cabinet.

"Here. Take two and put the rest in your purse." I held out the bottle of pain relievers. "Do you have enough pads, or do you need me to go get you some more?"

She gave me a small smile. "I'm fine, Mama Sensual."

"I'm just trying to make sure you are alright."

"I know, and I appreciate it. Now are you gonna be up under Denim all day, or do you wanna meet me at the Chinese place for lunch?"

I smacked my lips. "I do not be under him all day!"

"Maybe not all day, but everyday. Friday, Saturday, Sunday, and yesterday."

"Eleisha, why are you starting with me?!"

She giggled. "Because it's funny. You should see your face."

"You irk my nerves." I grinned. "But, yeah, I'll meet you. One o'clock?"

***

"See, I'm so confused, I just don't know what to do, and I don't understand, no..." I swayed and sang off key along with Meelah from 702 while chopping my seasonings for Christmas dinner.

Denim's laughter stopped me in my tracks. I spun around, and he was sitting at the kitchen table.

"How the hell? What the hell?!"

"I been sitting here for about three minutes. I knocked and rang the doorbell, but you didn't hear me. And the door was wide open."

I carried the container of my trinity to the fridge. "Yeah, I wanted to let some fresh air in."

"What you cooking?"

"Nothing. I'm just prepping for our Christmas meal. Tomorrow I'll make my gumbo and stuff before I come to your house."

"Gumbo and what stuff? What's gon' be on your menu?"

"I'm making gumbo, potato salad, cookies, pecan candy, and sweet potato pone." I placed the cutting board into the sink and washed my hands.

He nodded. "That sounds good."

"You hungry now? I can make you a sandwich or something."

"Naw. I'm good. I just wanted to see your face and let you know that I finished your book."

I leaned against the counter. "And?"

"It was aight." He grinned. "I stayed up until about one. I couldn't go to sleep without finishing it."

"Aight my ass! You know my stuff is fire!" I bragged.

"It is. I know that poetry is too. When you gon' let me read it?"

"I don't know, Denny. That's like letting you in on my deepest, most private thoughts. That's embarrassing."

"But you shared the other ones with the world."

"You want a cold drank or something?" I offered.

He chuckled. "No, I don't want a cold drank while you trying to change the subject."

I sighed. "Those were the mild ones, and I shared those because I thought- Look, since you really want to read my poems, I'll give you my notebook on January first."

What's the worst that could happen, other than him seeing how I still felt about him? At least it would be out in the open.

"Good because I'm trying to get all inside your mind."

You can get inside of something else too. I thought.

His phone chimed. "I gotta go take care of some last minute Christmas stuff."

I trailed behind him to the door.

"See you later, Chocolate." He kissed my cheek.

Closing and locking the door, I headed to my bedroom to get a quick nap in.

***

"Lord Jesus! Denim done put your ass to sleep!" EJ blared.

I rubbed my eyes to clear my vision. "What?" Assuming I'd missed lunch, I apologized, "I'm sorry, EJ! I overslept."

She plopped down beside me. "Girl, what are you talking about? It's just noon."

"Well, what are you doing here?"

"To make a long story short, me and my rude manager exchanged words. Talking about if it wasn't for Rozlyn, she would've been gotten rid of me, so I politely said "Ma'am, fuck you and this job."

"Eleisha!" I gasped. "You know she's gonna tell mama."

"I beat her to the punch. Mama and Andrew told me not to worry about it. Plus I have someone that's gonna plug me into a work-from-home job at the beginning of next month."

"At least you have a backup plan, and if you need me to help you out until then, you know I will."

She grinned slyly. "I still got a taste for Chinese food, but you can pay for it since I'm unemployed."

"Alright." I laughed. "Come on here, crazy girl."

***

"You wanna ride down the road with me, or is it gonna be too much for you?" EJ glanced over at me as she navigated her car onto our street after lunch.

"We can go," I replied.

She tooted her horn at a few of our neighbors.

"The hurricane really did a number on this street. This end looks like a warzone," I commented.

She pulled into the second entrance of the graveyard. "Yeah, but those houses were neglected and falling apart way before then."

"In the words of mama, "a shame before God." I exited and followed her to the trunk.

"All of these are for Bran?" There were four flower arrangements.

"No. I'm taking two to him and the other two to someone else, but you can go ahead and grab them. We'll walk to the other side and burn off some of these calories."

We trekked the few feet to Brandon's grave.

"Bran, look what I got for Christmas this year!" she exclaimed. "Tell God I said thank you." She turned and smiled at me.

"Aww, EJ," I gushed.

When she'd situated the flowers, she kissed her hand and touched the vault.

"You ready to go to the other side?"

I gave Brandon's resting place one last glance. "Yeah."

She led us to a pink vault on the other side of the cemetery. There was no headstone or any type of marker.

"Who's buried here?" I asked.

"Mrs. Sibley, the best teacher in the world." She beamed. "I loved me some Mrs. Sibley. I don't know what I would've done without her."

Looking around at all these graves was making me sad, but not EJ.

"I don't understand you, Eleisha," I stated.

She peered at me from her squatting position. "What don't you understand?"

"Being back here is dampening my mood, but you seem so unfazed. How come it doesn't bother you?

"It doesn't bother me as much because of this lady right here. Mrs. Sibley is the one who helped me get through my grief after what happened to Brandon. She made me realize that death is not the end. The physical body dies but not the spirit." She arranged her flowers and a few of the others that were already there. "You know what else she taught me that may help you in the future?"

"What's that EJ?"

"You remember when I was too sad to go to my graduation?"

"Mhmm." I nodded.

"She came to the house with my diploma, and we had a talk. She let me know that it's okay to grieve and be sad, but she also said that I shouldn't wallow in it and allow it to make me blind to all the other great things in my life."

"Mrs. Sibley sounds like a great woman. I'm glad you had somebody like her." I stooped to rub her back.

"Me too."

***

EJ stuck her head in the doorway. "Miss Sensual, do you mind putting that notebook down for a while and watching a movie with me?"

"Yes, ma'am." I chortled. "Do you wanna read what I wrote?"

"You volunteering to let lil ole me read your stuff?! A blizzard must be coming through!"

I smacked my lips. "It's not like your nosy ass don't be trying to sneak and read my stuff anyway."

I passed her the notebook and watched her expression change as she read the poem I'd written about how I loved and admired her.

"Choc..." Her eyes watered.

"You like it?"

"I love it!" She threw her arms around me, almost knocking me over. "Can I keep it? I wanna put it in a frame."

"Sure. Do you want me to type it up and print it out for you?"

"Nope. I want it like it is, in your handwriting."

I carefully tore the sheet from the notebook. "Here you go."

"I'll be right back." She kissed my cheek and ran off to her room.

***

I yawned as the ending credits of National Lampoon's Christmas Vacation rolled. "Alright, EJ. It's time to go to bed. We have a pretty busy day tomorrow."

"You're the one who wants to make gumbo and everything else under the sun." she said.

"So you not gonna help me tomorrow?"

"I'mma help, but I'm just saying." She stood up and stretched.

"Good night, girl." I chuckled.

Chapter 12

I'd awakened bright and early to deliver Christmas candies and the books that I'd promised Shanice. Now I was back at home making the roux for my gumbo while EJ cut up the potatoes for the potato salad. Pausing for a second, she answered her ringing phone.

"Hey, girls! What y'all doing?" mama asked.

"Hey, ma! We in here starting Christmas dinner," EJ responded.

"Jesus be a chef, a firefighter, and a roll of tissue," she quipped.

I hollered in laughter. "Ma, you know you're wrong for that!"

"I could've whipped up something when I made it in."

"We know, ma, but we don't want you to. Me and EJ got this."

"Yeah, ma! We got this. This is gonna be the best Christmas meal you ever had!" EJ co-signed.

She smiled. "Alright, girls! I'mma see what ya'll working with."

"What you been doing, ma?"

"Just finished double checking my bags. We'll be leaving out this evening, so I'll be back home sometime in the morning."

"So I only got a few hours of freedom left," EJ kidded. "Then it's back to the clank."

"Whatever, EJ," mama chuckled. "What you got planned anyway?"

"I'm going to Chris' sister's Christmas party."

"Choc, you going too?" mama questioned.

"No, ma'am. I have other plans," I responded.

EJ made a circle with her thumb and index finger before demonstrating the sex signal. "She's spending the evening with her Denny!" I popped her shoulder with the wooden spoon. "Oww!"

"Mmph... Well, you girls have fun, and please return the same way you left. Safe and, Eleisha, no babies!"

"Ma..." I laughed.

"I'mma let ya'll get back to your cooking. Call me if you need me to walk you through anything."

"Ok. Love you!" We chimed.

***

It seemed like we'd spent the majority of the morning stirring. EJ and I'd been alternating. We were now tackling the pecan candy.

Through the kitchen window, I peeped Denim's car pulling into our driveway.

"EJ, go open the door for Denim."

She hopped up with a grin on her face.

"Hey, bro!" I heard her speak. "She's in the kitchen. You can come in."

She entered with him trailing behind her, toting two twelve packs of cold dranks.

"Hey, Denny!" I smiled.

He placed the drinks on the kitchen table. "What's up, Chocolate? Y'all got it smelling good in here!"

"Chocolate, huh?" EJ smirked. "You know what they say about that?"

I cut my eyes at her, hoping she'd shut her trap.

"It's better to let it melt in your mouth and not in your hand." Denim ran his tongue over his lips. "Trust me, I know."

My mouth hit the floor as EJ snickered.

"I just came by to drop off these drinks. I'll be back to get you at about seven. Wear your fancy Christmas pajamas. I know you got some."

"Thank you, and okay. I'll see you later."

EJ grinned. "Thank you, Denim. I'll walk you out."

"Y'all are welcome." He eyeballed me before following EJ.

She returned to the kitchen grinning mischievously. "Is it just me, or does Denim seem to be applying slight pressure?"

Ignoring her, I spooned portions of the pecan candy onto a wax paper lined baking sheet.

"You don't have to answer me, but you know he was flirting with you."

"EJ, hush."

She continued, "Are you excited about spending Christmas Eve with him? I wonder what he has planned."

"Yes, but we'll probably just eat and watch movies," I responded.

"Maybe, maybe not. You wanna listen to some music?"

"Yeah, Christmas carols."

"Alright. I got the perfect song for you." She pressed play on her phone, and Betty Wright's "Tonight Is The Night" blasted from the bluetooth speaker that sat on the countertop.

"Really, EJ?!" I hollered. "How do you even know this song?"

"Your mama put me on to this, but I think this one is about you." She twittered.

"You know, you really make me sick!" I grabbed an oven mitt and chunked it at her.

***

"Which pajama set?" I asked EJ.

"I like the red button down one."

"Makeup or no makeup?"

She groaned. "Oh my God, Choc! You act like this is your first time celebrating a holiday with a man."

I cast my eyes downward. "I haven't spent Christmas Eve with a man since I left here, so I'm nervous."

"But you had a-"

"I know, I know. I don't wanna talk about it or think about it." I interrupted. "Will you please just help me?"

"Your skin is already gorgeous, so I say light eyeshadow and lip gloss. For your hair, a pineapple bun. Rub some Shea butter on the rest of that melanin and spray a little fragrance, you'll be good to go."

"Thank you." I smiled.

"You're welcome. I need to start getting ready myself." She headed in the direction of her room.

***

After getting dressed and doing my hair and makeup, I gave myself the once over in my full length mirror.

EJ barged in, putting a pair of large gold hoops in her ears. "Miss Sensual, why do you have that shirt buttoned all the way up to your neck?"

She came over and undid the top three buttons. "We need to add a little sex appeal to your look. I think you should remove that bra and knot your top, and take off those granny panties. I can see the lines under your shorts."

"EJ..." I whined.

"What?! Choc, at least give the man something to look at. You're going from Miss Sensual to Miss Prude."

"I am not a prude!"

"Mmph... I can't tell!" She shot back.

I quickly undressed, removed my undergarments, and let her fix my top.

"See that makes a big difference. You look great!" She passed me a small jewelry box. "Now put these on."

Opening the box, I found two heart shaped studs.

"Thank you, baby doll!" I wrapped my arms around her neck. "I have a gift for you too."

I went to my closet and pulled out the gift wrapped shoebox. "Here you go."

She sat on the bed and tore away the wrapping paper. Her eyes enlarged when she opened the box.

"Oh my God!" she gasped. "These are some bad ass shoes! Thank you, Choc!"

"I'm glad you like them."

"Like them?! I love them! I'm wearing these tonight!"

The doorbell chimed.

"That's probably your man," she stated. "I'll go let him in."

I slid my feet into my reindeer house slippers and grabbed my bag.

"Hey, Denny!" I smiled, sauntering into the living room. "I just gotta grab something out of the kitchen, and we can go."

"Damn, Chocolate!" He ran his tongue over his bottom lip as his eyes traveled from my open top to the hem of my bottoms that stopped at the top of my thighs.

"Excuse me for just a second, Denim," EJ said while following close on my heels.

"Girl, he's slobbering!" she sniggered. "Mission accomplished!"

"Girl..." I giggled while grabbing the bag of goodies and a bottle of wine.

"I want all the deets when you come back!"

"I'm not telling you all my business."

"Yes, you are!" she argued.

"Girl, I'm not about to stand here and play with you. I gotta go."

She grabbed my arm as I walked around her.

"Wait! Have fun tonight and don't do anything I wouldn't do." She grinned before kissing my cheek. "Merry Christmas Eve!"

I gave her a squeeze. "Merry Christmas Eve, Eleisha! You have fun too. I'll see you later tonight."

"Alright. I'm ready," I announced as I returned to the living room.

"See you later, EJ." He waved.

"See you later," she replied, walking us to the door and closing it behind us.

***

"You just gon' stand in the doorway?" Denim chortled.

I finally managed to pick up my jaw. "This... You did all this?"

"I told you it was gonna be special."

The lighting was low, making the Christmas lights that he'd strung along the walls one of the focal points. Ornaments and snowflakes hung from the ceiling, and in one corner of the room larger ornaments hung to form the shape of a Christmas tree. Christmas carols played softly in the background as the smell of gingerbread filled the air.

My mushy behind struggled to hold back tears.

"Come put your stuff down, so we can eat," he instructed.

I handed him the bottle of wine and bag of pralines and cookies before sitting my purse on the couch.

As we entered the kitchen, a guy in an apron was plating up food. Denim led me to the dining room table that was set up beautifully with a holiday bouquet as the centerpiece. My heart swelled as he pulled out my chair, and I couldn't hold back my tears.

"Denny, this is beautiful. I- No one has," I babbled.

He lifted my chin with his index finger and placed the softest kiss on my lips. "Well, I just did. Stop crying and enjoy."

Once we were seated, the chef brought over plates of lobster, asparagus, and garlic butter potatoes. The food rivaled that of some of the most expensive restaurants that I'd been to.

"This is so good."

"I know," Denim agreed. "I'm surprised you ain't over there moaning."

"I'm saving it for a more appropriate occasion." I giggled. "I still can't believe you hired a chef and did all this."

"It's Christmas Eve and date night. Gotta do it big."

A smile quivered on my mouth. "So this is a date?"

"Yes, Choc. This is a date, but you already knew that." His eyes landed on my ample bosom, and he caught his bottom lip between his teeth for a second. "Look at how you're dressed. You know exactly what you be doing."

"Actually, I just wanted to be cute." I raised my glass to my lips and took a sip of wine. "I don't know shit unless you clarify it."

"Okay." His dark irises held onto mine. "From this day forward, I'll make sure my intentions are crystal clear."

"I appreciate it." I grinned. "But I'm loving this date. You sure know how to make a girl feel special."

The chef approached the table. "Are ya'll ready for dessert?"

"You can just bring out one serving," Denim stated.

He returned a few moments later. "For your dessert, I've prepared some baked pears. I hope you enjoy."

"Thank you." I grinned until I realized that Denim was sliding the dish closer to his side of the table. "I guess I don't get any."

He sliced a piece and speared it with his fork. "We gon' share it. Here, you get the first bite."

My eyes closed involuntarily as my lips wrapped around the fork and fruit. "Mmm..." I pulled back and chewed slowly.

When I swallowed and opened my eyes, his low eyes were trained on my lips.

"My bad, Denny! But this is so good."

Shaking his head, he tasted a piece and mocked me. "Yeah, it's straight."

"You know, sometimes I don't like you." I laughed.

"You can have the last two bites, and then we'll do something else."

***

"Man, look at our gingerbread house!" I cackled.

"It's ugly as hell!" He laughed.

We'd tried our best, but it was a catastrophe. The house leaned slightly to the left, and the windows that I'd piped on were uneven.

"I don't ever wanna forget this. Let's take some pictures." I skittered to the living room to get my phone.

I took a couple of shots of our house before setting a timer for selfies. "Come on, Denny. Time to get your GQ on and drive the girls crazy."

"Hold up! If we gon' do a photoshoot, we gotta do it right." He grabbed a vase to prop the phone against and a chair. "Now, come sit in my lap."

We did a few poses in the chair, and for the final shot, I stood behind him and wrapped my arms around his neck.

"These are beautiful." I commented as I scrolled through them. "I'm gonna print them out and frame them."

"Don't forget to send them to me."

"I just sent them." I closed the app and locked my phone. "So what's next? We building a snowman?"

"Shid, if I knew where to find some snow I would've got that too." He chuckled. "But we just gon' chill and watch one of them mushy movies that you like. That's cool?"

"Yeah, but first, I have to use your restroom."

***

For a moment, I stared at my reflection in the mirror, feeling like I was dreaming. Not wanting to keep Denim waiting too long, I washed and dried my hands and checked my teeth.

"You good?" he asked as I made my way over to the couch.

"Yeah." I plopped down beside him.

"Before we start the movie, I wanna do something right quick." He pivoted to the right.

"Do what?"

"Merry Christmas, Chocolate." He handed me a small box.

"What is this? Denim, you said we weren't exchanging gifts!"

"Right, and we're not. I never said I wasn't getting you anything. Now open it."

I unwrapped the box and found a necklace with a quarter sized pendant that had one of the last pictures he, Brandon, and I'd taken together printed on it.

"Denim..." My eyes swam with tears. "Thank you. I love it."

"You're welcome." He smiled while passing me another gift.

"This is too much." The floral print on an Italian leather journal peeked out as I tore away the wrapping paper. "I should've gotten you something."

"Choc, you don't get it, do you?"

My face scrunched. "Get what?"

"You are the gift. You spending the evening with me is the gift." He handed me one more thing. "Last one."

I opened it and began flipping through the photo album that was inside. First there were pictures of him, my brother, and I as children. Next, there were pics of us in junior high and high school. Then I made it to a page of printed out text messages.

Bran: I been peeping some shit.

Denim: Peeping what?

Bran: The way you be looking at Choc, that's what. Like you like her or something.

Denim: Man...

Bran: Man nothing! You tried to holler at her?

Denim: No.

Bran: Why not?

Denim: Because it's Choc.

Bran: Scary ass! *laughing face emoji* I think she likes you too. I'd rather her be with you than anybody else. Shoot yo shot nigga!

The pages that followed were filled with pictures of us that we'd taken over the three year course of our relationship. Underneath the last photo was a note. **To be continued... Yes? No?**

I placed the album beside me on the couch and lifted my eyes to meet his.

"So?" He waited for my response.

"Yes," I whispered.

His mouth crashed into mine, drawing a moan, as his tongue slipped between my lips.

Pulling away from our tongue dance, I breathed, "Denny... let's go to your room."

He'd said I was the gift, so I was gonna let him unwrap me. He didn't respond verbally, but his lust filled eyes screamed "say less."

***

My heart thumped rapidly as he laid me back on his navy blue bedding and loosened the knot of my blouse. He peppered kisses from my lips to my plump mounds, stopping to swirl his tongue around my dark nipples and areolas.

"Denim..." My back arched as he suckled my nipple and pinned it lightly between his teeth.

"You like that?" he whispered.

"Mhmm..." I moaned.

He latched onto one like he was trying to nurse, making me cry out. My body had a mind of its own as my legs wrapped around his torso and my hips began to wind. The sensation from his mouth and the friction of the seam of my shorts against my clit had my juices seeping through the satin material.

"Damn, you wet as hell," he muttered before sliding his tongue down my stomach and dipping it into my belly button.

He raised up, removed my bottoms, kissed, and licked up my legs until he was face to face with my center. Pushing my legs back, he played in my wetness with his fingers.

"Dennnyyyy..." I whined as his index and middle fingers moved in and out of me.

"I want you to cum in my mouth," he stated, removing his fingers to envelop my entire vulva with his thick lips. His tongue swiped between my inner and outer labia, teasing me, and then flickered rapidly against my clit. Soon, my thighs had him in a headlock as my stomach and vaginal muscles contracted. His stiff tongue entered my hole, catching every drop of my honey.

As I laid there shaking like a leaf on a windy fall afternoon, he stood up to remove his bottoms, revealing the gift that I knew would keep on giving. He stroked his slightly curved inches while sliding back into position between my quivering legs. He ran his mushroom shaped tip back and forth against my sensitive clit and labia until my juices splashed his abdomen. Not giving me a second to catch my breath, he plunged into me and let out a hiss. "Fuck, Choc..."

I pulled his bottom lip into my mouth, tasting my essence, as he began to slide in and out of me slowly. Forehead to forehead, we stared into each other's eyes and chanted each other's names simultaneously. My legs wrapped around his waist, and I met every stroke he delivered. We rocked and rolled until our skin became slick with sweat. They say sex is spiritual, and I believe it. Tonight, our souls reconnected.

***

We'd been going at it so much that I didn't know what round this was. My head rested in the crook of Denim's neck as he slid his arms around my legs until the back of my knees rested in the crook of his elbows. With his hands cupping my buttocks, he slammed me up and down on his penis.

"I- Oooh- oh my God! Please!"

"Yeah, Choc! Scream for me, just like that!" He grunted while raising his pelvis to pound into me.

"Denim, please! I can't!" I wailed.

"Yes, you can. You taking it so well."

Our thighs became sticky as he continued to pummel into me.

"That's right, Chocolate. Cum on it," he groaned. "I'm bout to cum in a second, ok?"

"O-ok!"

He let out a growl, releasing his seeds.

***

"You soaked my bed. We gon' have to sleep in one of the other rooms," Denim said while cleaning me gently.

"Alright." I yawned, struggling to move.

Chuckling, he scooped me up bridal style and carried me down the hallway. I read the digital clock on the nightstand. 5:45 a.m. He tucked me underneath the covers and snuggled against me.

"Merry Christmas." He placed a gentle kiss on the nape of my neck. "I love you, Choc."

"Merry Christmas, and I love you too, Denny," I replied before letting sleep take over.

***

"Ma, I'm coming!" I heard Denim speak as I rubbed sleep from my eyes. "Them ain't my kids! I don't have to be there for them to open up their gifts! I'm about to shower, and then I'll be on my way. Alright. Bye. Love you too."

He noticed that I was awake. "Good morning, beautiful!"

"Beautiful?" I croaked. "I look like shit, but good morning."

"I'm about to brush my teeth and hop in the shower. You wanna join me?"

I sat on the edge of the bed and stretched. "Yeah."

***

I emptied my bladder as he applied toothpaste to two brushes.

"Damn, Chocolate! It sounds like you over there frying chicken," he teased.

I unrolled some tissue and patted my swollen nether region softly. "You make me sick."

I washed my hands before grabbing the toothbrush.

"What?" I asked as he stared at me.

"Nothing," he grinned, shifting his focus to the mirror and brushing his teeth.

After brushing and rinsing, we stepped into the shower. He pressed his semi-hard manhood against my buttcheeks as the stream of warm water rained down on us. His hands cupped my D-cups, tweaking my nipples before traveling down my toned stomach to the heat between my legs, where his fingertips found my love button.

Bad as I wanted him to penetrate me, I knew I wouldn't be able to function if I let him inside again. I pushed his hands away and turned around to face him. "I can't. I'm too sore."

"Okay." He nodded his understanding and lowered his head to kiss me.

He couldn't penetrate me, but that didn't mean that I couldn't help him get off.

Suckling his tongue, I reached down and wrapped my hand around his thickness. I tightened my grip just a little and stroked it at a steady pace while reaching underneath to massage his scrotum. His husky moans let me know that it felt good. My mouth trailed from his soft lips to one of man's most erogenous zones, his nipples.

"Aww, fuck, Choc." He threw his head back as I flickered my tongue.

Seeing his reaction caused me to drip like a faucet. He caressed my body blindly until his hand found its way between my legs. His thumb made rapid circular motions against my clitoris as I continued to jack him off. The sounds of our moans bounced off the walls as we made it closer to the finish line. Reaching my climax, my mouth formed an O. Denim panted, unable to steady his breathing, as his hot semen shot out onto my stomach.

***

We kissed sloppily as his car idled in the street in front of my driveway. Pulling back, he checked his ringing phone. "That ain't nobody but my mama. I gotta get going, Chocolate. I'll be back tomorrow night."

"Alright." I nodded. "Tell Ms. Dana nem I said Merry Christmas."

"To be honest, I really don't want to leave you."

"Denny, go see your mama." I chuckled. "I'll still be here when you get back."

"Gimme another kiss." He grabbed my face, tracing my tender lips with the tip of his tongue.

Chapter 13

EJ sat on the couch waiting for me like a strict parent.

"Well, well, well... Look what the cat dragged in! You look like pure d shit but in a good way. I take it the night went well."

"Why thank you!" I yawned. "And it did. The night and the morning."

I yawned again. "I'm gonna go take a quick nap before mama gets here."

"Okay. And Merry Christmas, floozy." A smile crept up on her face.

"Merry Christmas, Eleisha!"

My sore muscles carried me down the hallway and to my bed. Within minutes, I was fast asleep.

***

The smell of gumbo wafted through the air into the living room as mama stood over the pot stirring. EJ and I busied ourselves cleaning up the wrapping paper and bows that littered the floor.

Suddenly, there was a knock at the door.

"Mama, are you expecting company?" I questioned.

"No. I don't know who that is. Just answer it," she called.

I placed the paper into a large trash bag before heading to the door as they continued to knock. Not peeping to see who it was, I flung the door open.

"Brandon!" I gasped, jumping up and wrapping my arms and legs around his torso, causing him to drop the gifts that he held. "What are you doing here?"

He placed a kiss on my cheek. "Merry Christmas, Choc! You know I wasn't gonna let the day go by without coming to see y'all."

"Oh my God! Mama, look!" EJ screamed.

"What, EJ?!" She rushed from the kitchen. "Oh my God! My baby!"

They ran out onto the porch, and we all cried and shared a group hug.

***

Even in my sleep, I could smell my mama's perfume.

"Choc!" She peppered my face with kisses as her tears dampened my jaws.

"Mama..." I mumbled. Although it was a struggle, I finally pulled myself from dreamland. "Mama!"

I sat up and squeezed her tight.

She laid her head on my shoulder and cried harder. "My baby... I'm so happy to see you!"

"Aww, ma!" My own tears started to flow as we held each other and rocked.

"Are y'all gonna sit there glued at the bosom all day? Me and Andrew are hungry!" EJ leaned against the doorframe.

"Oh, yeah! Andrew," mama said like it'd slipped her mind that he even existed. "Come on so you can meet him."

"I need a minute to make myself presentable." My hair was all over my head, and I still had on my pajamas.

She pressed the back of her hand to my forehead. "You've been sleeping all day? Are you feeling well?"

"I'm fine. Just had a long night."

"I bet."

"Ma...." I guffawed. "Gimme ten minutes."

***

I changed into an Elk and heart print jumpsuit and fixed my puff before heading into the living room.

"There she is!" Mama grinned.

"Bout time," EJ mumbled.

"Choc, this is Andrew, my special someone! Andrew, this is Choc!"

I could tell by her demeanor that she was really smitten. He rose to his feet to shake my hand, or so I thought. Reaching out, he pulled me close to his tall frame, and even though this man was a complete stranger, I wasn't uncomfortable.

"Nice to finally meet you, although I feel like I already know you." He flashed perfectly aligned teeth.

Mama beamed beside him.

"Nice to meet you too, and I've heard a few things about you as well." I smiled.

"Ole EJ, you put in a good word for me?" He turned towards her and grinned.

She held out her fist for a bump. "Of course. You my dawg."

Mama shook her head. "Y'all wanna open presents or eat first?"

"Eat!" EJ blared. "I already warmed up the food. Presents don't help hunger."

We all filed into the kitchen where mama and her man had a seat at the table. EJ and I grabbed bowls from the cabinets and dipped up the gumbo.

"Y'all want potato salad too?" I asked.

"I want whatever y'all got," Andrew answered. "And I hope it tastes as good as it smells."

"Sure. And like I said before, Jesus please be a roll of toilet tissue," mama quipped.

"Don't start that mess!" I twittered while sitting her food in front of her. I went to the fridge to survey our drink choices. "We got water, Coke, and a bottle of wine. Take your pick."

"We'll take a glass of wine," mama stated.

"Me too," EJ chimed.

I smacked my lips. "You are not even old enough. You're still wet behind the ears."

"See you... You lucky Drew is here..." Walking with earshot of me, she narrowed her eyes. "And you still walking around with a wet ass," she whispered.

"Silly!" I rinsed out four wine glasses and filled them.

When we were all settled around the table, we clasped hands as Andrew led the prayer. "Bless the food before us, the family beside us, and the love between us. Amen."

"Amen!"

We began to dig in.

"Roz, this gumbo is almost as good as yours," he commented.

"I taught my girls well," she bragged.

I smirked. "Uh-Uh, don't be tryna ride our coattails now!"

"Mhmm... Like she ain't try to shade us a minute ago!" EJ added.

"Oooh, they on your ass, baby." Andrew teased.

"I ain't worried about them chaps, and it's still gotta digest." She stuck her tongue out at us, making us all laugh.

"Choc, I heard you need a car," he stated.

"Yeah, I do. You know where I can get a good deal?" I blew my gumbo before putting it in my mouth.

"I got one, a black 2017 Honda Accord."

"How much do you want for it?"

"Nothing." He shrugged.

"Nothing?!" I gasped. "Why you wanna just give it away? You don't even know me like that."

"I don't need the money, and I know enough. I'd rather you have it than for it to just be sitting up."

"But I don't feel right accepting it for nothing. You gotta let me pay you something."

"Two hundred dollars then."

"Two hundred dollars?!" I exclaimed. "That ain't enough!"

"Look, Choc, either way it's gon' end up parked in this yard." He sipped from his glass of wine as mama gazed at him all googly eyed.

"I'll give it to you before you leave."

***

"EJ, what in the world?" I hurriedly stashed the rose toy in the gift bag with the dresses she'd gotten me. "Why would you get me this?!"

Her laughter rang out. "I got that the day after you came back. I thought you might need it."

"What did you get?" mama asked, trying to peek into the bag.

"You don't want to know." I passed a present to her and Andrew. "This is for you, and this is yours."

"Thank you, baby." She leaned over and kissed my temple.

"Aww, you got something for me too! Thank you." Andrew beamed.

"Of course. Can't leave you out."

His eyes lit up as he opened the Christmas card and the gift card to his favorite food spot. "This sholl gon' come in handy next time I hit the road."

"Fendi frames! I love these!" mama gasped. "My half blind ass is taking these to my ophthalmologist Monday!"

"Here, EJ! This last gift is yours!"

She snatched it out of my hand and ripped it open. "A pandora bracelet like yours!" She got up and sprinkled wet kisses on my face.

"Get off me, lil girl!" I joked.

Gathering up my gifts, I stood to take them to my room.

I sat them on the bed, got Andrew's money, and headed back to the living room.

"I gotta go check on things at home." He and mama stood to their feet.

"Thank you for everything, Andrew. Here's your money." I passed it to him.

"You're welcome, Choc. I'll see y'all later."

"See you later, Drew." EJ smiled.

Mama walked him to the door, and he tried to discreetly slide the money to her before pulling her close and kissing her passionately. Blushing, she quickly glanced back at us.

***

Mama had a seat on my bed as I finished setting up my oil diffuser. "So what do you think about Andrew?"

"He's nice. I like him, and I like him for you." I plopped down beside her. "The fact that you brought him around us says a lot."

I couldn't recall a man being in this house since she divorced EJ's father, and that was when I was around eight. I know she had boyfriends, but they never made it to the point of being introduced to us. She and I had plenty of talks about relationships as I got older, and one thing I knew about mama was that she didn't put up with bullshit. And she always stressed how important it was to not have a bunch of men running in and out of your house, especially when you're raising girls.

She tilted her head. "You know, it's really different with him. We became great friends before anything else, and that man was a Godsend for me and EJ. Now my ass is in love."

"I can tell, and I love that for you." I smiled.

She noticed the pendant on my necklace and lifted it up. "This is beautiful. Where'd you get this?"

"It's one of my Christmas gifts from Denim. I gotta show you my other stuff." I got up and grabbed the journal and photo album from the dresser.

"This is a nice journal." She put it down and flipped through the photo album. "Aww, look at my babies."

"Ma, why did you comb my hair like that?" I asked.

She laughed. "Girl, I did the best I could. You were still cute."

Continuing to flip, she made it to the messages between Denim and Brandon. "Aww... Brandon gave his blessing. This is the sweetest thing I've ever seen. Look at you and Denim. You can just see the love." She made it to the last page. "To be continued... Yes or No. I'm guessing you and Denim are..."

"Yes, ma'am." I grinned. "Things are still the same."

"I figured it would be that way."

"Mama, sometimes I wonder where we'd be if I wouldn't have left."

She wrapped her arm around me and rubbed my shoulder. "Choc, sometimes life separates people in order for them to grow, but if they're meant to be, it also brings them back together. Don't dwell on it."

"Yes, ma'am." I rested my head on her shoulder.

***

I laid under the covers talking to Denim over the phone.

"I wish you was in this bed with me," he said.

"To do what?" I quirked a black eyebrow. "I'm in bad shape right now."

"To cuddle, crazy girl. It ain't gotta be all that."

"I know that, Denny."

He ran his tongue over his lips and grinned slyly. "But I have a house now. We can get it on and poppin' all over that muthafucka!"

"Denim, what is wrong with you?!" I covered my mouth so I wouldn't laugh too loud.

"Nothing, just thinking about that chocolate, but I'mma hush about it." He chuckled. "Tell me what you got for Christmas."

"I got dresses, candles, and a desk. Oh, & I got a car."

"A car?"

"Andrew gave it to me. I'm still shocked by that, especially since today was my first time meeting him."

"That's because the man loves your mama, and she's probably told him a few things about you."

"And I forgot. I got a man named Denim for Christmas too," I teased.

"Damn!" he huffed. "I did all that extra stuff for nothing then."

"Nah, that was one of the best things I've ever experienced. I'll never forget last night. Thank you, Denim." My voice cracked with emotion.

"That was just the beginning. I can finally afford to treat you to things like I want to."

"I don't really care about all that. I mean it's nice, but I loved you when we both were broke as a joke. I still do."

"I know, and I love you too."

***

Apryl and I'd been missing each other's calls for the past two days, but I was finally able to catch up with her.

"Hey, heifer! What have you been doing where you couldn't answer my calls for Christmas Eve or Christmas?" She furrowed her brow.

"I spent Christmas Eve with Denim."

"And?!"

"I went home a new woman!" I exclaimed.

Her mouth formed an oval of surprise. "Ya'll had sex?!"

"Mhmm... All night long."

"Girlll..."

"Girlll...." I repeated before we both fell into a fit of giggles.

EJ barged into my room.

"Damn, EJ! Didn't mama teach you some manners?" I fussed.

"She did, but I get amnesia sometimes when it comes to you." She stood in front of me with her hand on her wide hip. "Drew just dropped off your car."

"Okay, but you see I'm on the phone! Dang!" I smacked my lips. "Apryl, do you want a sister?"

"She'll probably appreciate me more than you do." She jutted her bottom lip. "You been acting different since Denim put that wood to you."

Apryl shrieked on the other end.

I audibly gasped. "Get out of here, Eleisha, before I tell mama on you!"

"Really? At your big age!"

"EJ, get out of here!" I gritted.

"Bye, Choc! I love you!" She smiled, having accomplished her mission of getting on my nerves.

"Your sister is a mess!" Apryl cried.

"She gets on my nerves!" I tittered.

"I see you found a car. That was quick."

"A car found me. My stepdaddy gave it to me," I explained.

"I love how everything is coming together for you. You are one blessed chick."

"Indeed, I am," I agreed.

Chapter 14

"I'm surprised she's not somewhere laid up with her Denny," EJ teased as she, mama, and I dined at a Mexican restaurant. "She chose us today, so he must be busy."

"EJ, shut up." Mama laughed. "Don't you have Chris?"

Her face soured. "No! He gets on my nerves."

Mama's eyes rolled. "Here we go again."

"Whatever. He'll be on his knees ea-"

EJ cut me off with a fake cough.

"Choc, you look good, girl," Mama complimented. "You're glowing."

"I'm so happy to be home and around y'all, even though Eleisha is a thorn in my side. It's like I can breathe easier."

"Around us when?!" EJ scoffed.

"Don't play!" I glared. "You know we just took you out to eat with us the other day."

"Yeah and did all that touching and kissing. *Denny! Heehee! Stoppp!*" She imitated me. "Almost made me lose my appetite."

Mama clutched her abdomen as she hollered.

"It's not my fault that my man knows my love language and doesn't mind showing a little PDA. You know, they should put your picture in the dictionary right beside the word hater."

"He knows your what? And I'm never a hater. You know I've been team Denim and Choc since the day you arrived."

"I know. And love language is the way a person prefers to receive love from their partner," I elaborated. "There are five of them; words of affirmation, quality time, receiving gifts, acts of service, and physical touch. Mine are quality time and physical touch. What are yours?"

Her forehead creased as she thought. "I'd have to say quality time, physical touch, and receiving gifts. Ma, what are yours?"

"Words of affirmation, quality time, and acts of service. Physical touch is nice, but I'm too old to do all that hunching." She giggled.

"Oh my God!" I scoffed. "You act like you're ninety years old!"

EJ twisted her lips. "Girl, don't let mama fool you! I've heard a few things late at night!"

I screamed in laughter.

Mama's face turned beet red. "Are you serious?!"

"Mhmm..."

"Oh my goodness!" She cast her eyes downward.

EJ's eyes glimmered in amusement. "Don't be ashamed, Roz. In the words of Ezal from Friday, *I ain't gon' tell nobody else!*"

"I can't believe I birthed such a child."

Tears streamed down my face as my shoulders bounced. "I gotta go to the restroom!"

***

"Hello?" I answered my ringing phone as I made my way back to our table.

"Hey, baby!" Denim greeted. "What you doing?"

"I'm out with EJ and my mama. What you doing?"

"In the hardware store with Mr. Percy. Hold on. You can't get that one. It's not gon' fit."

"I don't like the way the other ones look!" I heard Mr. Percy say in the background. "I can make this one work."

"Man, get the right one cause we not bout to keep coming back to this store," Denim fussed before laughing along with me. "This don't make no sense. I don't know what's wrong with him."

"Y'all are a mess!" I tittered.

"Naw, he is a mess. Anyway, Chocolate, I was calling to tell you to put some cute shit on and be ready at 8. I'm taking you on a date."

"Mmph!" I grunted, pleased with his spontaneity. "Alright. I'll be ready at eight."

***

My mama and Denim's laughter carried down the hallway and into my bedroom as I applied the finishing touches on my makeup. Satisfied with my ensemble, I strutted into the living room in my five inch heels.

Lust flickered in Denim's dark brown eyes.

"Oooh! I knew that one would look good on you!" EJ complimented.

I was rocking one of the dresses she'd gifted me for Christmas; a mid-length black slinky tube number with a slit that ran up to where my leg and hip met.

"That is quite a dress." Mama eyed my attire. "You look great, sweetie."

"Thank you." I grinned while walking over to kiss her and EJ's cheek. "I'll probably see y'all tomorrow."

"Alright, my babies. Have fun."

"Yeah, have fun, and don't do anything that I wouldn't do," EJ added.

"Let's roll!" I pulled Denim out the door as he waved goodbye.

"You must not wanna make it off this porch, putting that shit on." His warm breath tickled my ear.

"We better because I didn't do all this for nothing. I'mma let you undress me later though."

***

Denim's hand crept closer to my honey pot as he massaged my creamy thigh.

"Choc, can we pull over for just a second? Please?" he begged.

"No, Denny!" I tittered. "You are not about to fuck me in this car and get us both all sweaty. You need to relax."

"How?! How you expect me to relax, Choc?!" he griped. "You know exactly what you be doing!"

I grinned devilishly because, indeed, I did. "Concentrate on the music that's playing or something."

He leaned forward to adjust the volume. "Yeah, aight! I'mma fix yo ass!"

***

"I've been thinking," Denim started as we finished our meal. "You know how you plan to start looking for an apartment soon?"

"Yeah."

"I think you should move in with me." He pressed his lips together, waiting for my response.

"Hmmm..." It wasn't such a bad idea. With my mama and EJ being right across the street, I'd still be at home.

"Look, Choc, I know about the situation you just left behind, but that's not how it's gonna be with us. Yes, I work long hours. But every second that I'm free, I wanna spend it with you." His eyes searched mine. "And I still wanna do all the things that we planned before you left."

"I do too. And I know that it's different with us." In my mind, the bond that I thought I'd shared with Calvin could never compare to the one I shared with Denim. "So yes, sir! I would love to take over your crib." I leaned forward and puckered my lips. "I love you, Denny."

"I love you too," he responded before kissing me.

"Aww... You guys are a beautiful couple," an older woman commented from another table.

My cheeks flushed a rosy hue. "Thank you."

"Denim, I'm going to the restroom."

***

"Girl, you see that dude in there?" a woman asked her friend as they entered the restroom.

"Which one?"

"Girl, it ain't but one fine muthafucka in there!"

"Oh yeah! I saw, but I think he's with somebody."

"Damn!" She smacked her lips. "You still wanna go to Sparkle when we leave here? It's poetry night."

"I guess."

My interest peaked at the mention of poetry night. After using my foot to flush the toilet, I emerged from the stall.

"Hi!" I spoke politely, making my way to the vanity to wash my hands.

"Hey!" The tall sista waved. "Girl, you are so pretty, and I love that dress."

"Thank you!" I beamed. "Listen, I don't mean to be all in your conversation, but where's this club that y'all were talking about?"

"You know where the university is?"

I nodded.

"It's right down the street."

"Okay. Thank you!" I grinned before heading towards the exit.

***

"Denim, do you mind if we make another stop? I wanna check something out." I slipped my arms into my cropped leather bomber jacket.

"Naw." He slid his keys across the table. "Where you trying to go?"

"This lil spot on University Ave. I wanna hear some poetry and dance."

He reached out and slapped my behind, making it jiggle as we exited the restaurant.

"Stoppp...." I whined.

The window of the car next to his rolled down, revealing the girl from the restroom. "Damn, chick! That's you?! Everybody ain't able!"

I flashed her a smile before climbing behind the wheel.

***

We found a nice spot where we could still see the stage in a corner of the dimly lit club.

"Last call for those participating in poetry night!" the DJ announced.

"You reciting your poetry?" Denim whispered. "It'll be a good way to promote your work."

"Hell no! I just came to admire other people's talent." I rocked my hips to some throwback Boosie.

The place was a vibe, mixing it up with old and new hip hop with some r&b mixed in between. As the track came to an end, the emcee made her way to the stage. "Let me hear you give it up if you ready for poetry night!"

Placing two fingers into my mouth, I let out a whistle.

"Alright, alright!" She glanced down at the paper in her hand. "I see we got some talent in here tonight! Coming to the stage first, we have Moonlight! Give it up for her!"

A petite woman with hair twice the size of mine strutted onto the stage. In her smooth melodic voice she recited a poem titled "Pussy Power." By the time she finished, she had all of us females feeling like we were toting around that platinum plus gushy. Next, a guy by the name of Mike B. hit the stage with a poem about men dropping the tough exterior and being raw.

Denim applauded loudly. "I like that one!"

Last, another woman by the name of Miss Virgo took to the stage and recited a poem about no good men, causing half of the club-goers to groan.

"If this poem offended you and you feel some type of way about me, then you probably one of the niggas mentioned. And I mean this from the bottom of my heart; fuck ya!" She flipped the bird and exited the stage.

"Damn! Who hurt sis?!" Denim snickered in my ear.

"I don't know, but she spit the real!" I laughed.

The emcee returned to the stage. "Give it up for our brave poets, Moonlight, Mike B., and the outspoken, Miss Virgo! If you enjoyed our poetry night, be sure to come check us out every Friday! Mr. DJ, let's groove!"

I reached up, pulling Denim's head closer to mine, and caressed his face as Nia Sultana's "Entirely" floated from the speakers. "Dance with me!"

"I can't dance, Chocolate!"

"Your sex game lets me know that you got good rhythm, so it's not like you can't dance! You just don't! Come on now! Just rock with me!"

He wrapped his arms around my waist and swayed with me.

I moved his hands when the beat of Chris Brown's "Under The Influence" dropped. Bending over, I placed my hands on my knees and whined my hips against him. Feeling him rising in his jeans, I bit my lip and got real nasty with it. He wrapped his hand around my neck, pulling me upward.

"Why you doing this shit to me?" he breathed into my ear before tilting my head back and sticking his tongue down my throat. He pulled away slightly. "I'm ready to go!"

***

Unwilling to make the drive home, we checked into a fairly decent hotel. I'd unzipped Denim's pants in the elevator, so it was on and popping when we made it into the room.

Yanking his bottoms down, I shoved him against the door and dropped to my knees. Staring up into his eyes, I gripped his veiny dick, slid my tongue between my wine colored lips, and traced the glans. Opening my mouth slightly, I sucked gently and french kissed it, darting my tongue into his urethral orifice. His pee hole, in simpler terms.

"Aaahhh…" he moaned while slipping his fingers into the curly tendrils on top of my head. "Fuck!"

I paused to lubricate my hand with saliva. Running my wet palm along his inches, my mouth concentrated on the tip. Soon, his legs and his penis began to twitch as his seeds spilled down my throat. He gripped the door frame to hold himself up.

I sat on the bed, watching him stumble over to a chair. In less than five minutes, he was back cocked and ready.

"No! Stay right there!" I instructed, slipping off my thong.

Gripping the arms of the chair, I slid down on him slowly and cried out. Something about being in reverse cowgirl made it hit different and deeper. I wasn't sure if I'd be able to take it, but I was gonna get an A for effort.

"Oooh, shit!" I groaned through gritted teeth.

Denim, the ever so encouraging freak, growled, "Yeah, Choc! Ride that shit!"

The pressure wasn't so bad as I got wetter, so I began to bounce faster and harder.

When he grunted, "Yes! Yes, baby! I love the way you fucking me!" I felt like a winner at the Kentucky Derby.

One of his hands gripped my throat while the other held onto one of my bouncing breasts.

"Denim..." I gasped. "I'm... about... to..."

"Aahhh... me too."

I rained down on him as he spouted in me.

***

Bent over with my dress around my abdomen like a scrunchie, I screamed at the top of my lungs. "Denim, why are you doing me like this?! You know your name is already stamped on it!"

"Shut the fuck up before you get us kicked out!" The slap he delivered sat my buttcheek on fire.

The way he was assaulting my kitty should've been a crime. Denim had the kind of dick that could either make my soul float or revive me. Right now, he was killing me. I crawled away in an attempt to lessen some of the pressure.

"Uh-uh! Don't run!" He grunted.

Reaching forward, he gripped my coiled strands and stretched my shrinkage. My legs could no longer support me after my third orgasm. I fell flat on my stomach in the middle of the wet spot as he continued to annihilate me. I don't know if he saw tonight as a sexing competition, but he'd won.

***

"Choc, are you okay?" He studied me with concern. "You not talking."

"I can't," I responded, barely audible.

"Damn! Your voice is gone." I watched his penis swing like a pendulum as he went to the microwave to heat up some water in one of the disposable cups. He brought the hot water over with a tea bag and a couple of packs of sugar. "I'm sorry. I didn't mean to hurt you."

"It's ok, Denny." I chuckled. "I'm fine. Might not be able to walk again, but I'm fine."

I drank the hot tea and slid underneath the covers.

"My name is stamped on it, huh?" he asked, his voice laced with amusement.

I pursed my lips. "Good night, sir."

"You alright?" Denim kissed the back of my hand as we headed home the following morning.

"Yes. Just thinking, that's all."

"Care to share?"

I trained my eyes on his perfect side profile. "It's just crazy to me how I'll be stepping into a new year here with y'all in a few hours. Things are still the exact same, but it's different. I don't know how to explain it. And us..."

His eyes darted in my direction and back to the road. "Time and distance doesn't affect real love. And as far as things being different, it ain't me, your mama, or your sister. It's you."

"What you mean?"

"You'll figure it out." He smiled. "Now, what do you wanna eat for breakfast?"

Chapter 15

"You look like a lady of the night." EJ began her shenanigans as I entered the house.

"Good," I quipped. "I certainly behaved like one."

She made an ugly face. "Eww!"

I made my way to the bathroom with her right on my heels. She flopped down on the toilet as I peeled off my dress. "Eleisha, what do you want?"

"I need to talk to my floozy of an older sister."

"EJ, is something wrong?" I grabbed the sides of her face and examined her.

"No, worrywart!" she laughed. "I just want the tea on last night since you came back with that dress turned inside out."

"I noticed it when I made it to the car this morning, but last night was fun. I found a nice lil spot for us to go to when we have girl's night next weekend."

"Girl's night?"

"Yeah, lovey! We bout to start turning up and enjoying ourselves." I stuck a toe in the water. It was nice and hot.

"Ok!" She grinned, reaching for a towel and lathering it with Dove mango and almond butter body wash. "I can't wait! I can't wait for tonight either. Ms. Dana throws the best kickbacks."

"Yeah. It'll probably be fun."

Denim's mother was having a small get together at his house to bring in the new year.

"You got a New Year's resolution, EJ?" I asked as she scrubbed my back.

"To reduce some of this fluff."

"That's one of mine." I chortled. "We can be workout partners."

She continued, "And to find my niche. I feel like I have no direction in life."

"EJ, you're only twenty. You're not supposed to have everything figured out. These are your life lesson years. Hell, look at me! I barely know anything!"

"Yeah, you are pretty slow!" She laughed as I flipped her the bird. "But, Miss Sensual, all jokes aside, I'm excited about what the new year is gonna be like now that you're back."

"Aww...me too." I smiled.

**

After getting dressed, I connected my phone to the charger and powered it. I'd missed several calls from Apryl last night, and there was a text telling me to call her back asap. I dialed her number twice, only to go to voicemail. A part of me started to think the worst. I checked her Facebook profile and didn't see anything alarming.

"She probably just wants to gossip," I mumbled.

Ready to get the ball rolling again with my writing career, I sat at my desk and emailed Samantha a copy of my book. She emailed me back within minutes. **Got it! Welcome back!**

I closed my laptop and reached for the journal that Denim gifted me. I'd decided to use it as a prayer and manifestation journal for the upcoming year. EJ burst into my room just as I finished jotting down my first goal.

"Oohwee, Choc! Your doctor man is outside!"

"Get out of here, Eleisha!" I fussed. "You see I'm trying to write! I don't have time to be playing with you!"

"I'm not playing! Go look!"

I hotfooted it to the living room window, and sure enough there was Calvin dressed in a red polo and khakis, holding a bouquet of roses.

"What the fuck?"

I took a second to smooth my wild hair and adjust the hem of my shorts before stepping onto the porch. "Calvin, what are you doing here?"

"I'm here because I love you and I need you, Liyah."

I suddenly felt like I'd been thrown into a sappy romance movie that I wanted no parts of. The sincerity was visible in his eyes, but still. I'd disposed of any remnants of love for him the night of the gala.

I exhaled loudly. "Cal-"

"I don't want to start the new year off without you. I know I haven't contacted you, but that's because I didn't want to step to you without having my shit together. The things you told me, nobody's ever said those things to me, and I've been thinking about it ever since. You were right." He reached out and grasped my hand.

"Calvin, it's too-"

"Listen to me, please." His Adam's apple bobbed. "I realized that I don't want to miss out on building a family, and I don't want to miss out on you. I resigned from the hospital. I'm starting a new job at a clinic, so I'll have more time for what matters."

"I'm sorry, but it's too late," I said softly.

His face dropped. "What do you mean it's too late? Liyah, it's only been two weeks."

"It's been two weeks since I left your home, but we've been separated mentally and emotionally for months." My eyes traveled across the road to Denim and his mother who were headed to his car.

"But we can get back to the way we were in the beginning. Baby, please don't do this," he pleaded.

Denim backed out his driveway and stopped in front of ours. "Hey, Chocolate! We bout to make a store run. You need anything?"

Calvin's eyes bounced between the two of us.

"Hey, Denny! Hey, Ms. Dana!" I called. "No thank you! I'm good!"

"Okay, baby! See you later." He flashed that perfect smile and drove off.

"Chocolate? Baby? Liyah, who is that?" Calvin queried.

"Cal, you have no right to be questioning me." My arms crossed underneath my breasts.

"I saw how he looked at you. Are you sleeping with him?!"

"That's none of your business."

"Two weeks, and you're already fucking somebody else!" His light complexion reddened, and his nostrils flared. "You're nothing but a slut!"

"Yes, Calvin!" Puffing out my chest, I took a step forward, getting all in his personal space. "I am a slut, and I'm letting him fuck the shit out of me! And you wanna know something else?! His dick is so much bigger and better than yours! It's so good that I don't want to even think about getting back with you! Goodbye!"

I went back inside and slammed the door behind me.

Breezing past a shocked EJ, I headed straight to my room.

"Choc!" she called from the other side of my door.

"Leave me alone, EJ."

"No can do." She entered the room snickering. "That was so terrible but so hilarious! I can't believe you said that! He's just now picking up his lip and leaving!"

"I hate to act ugly, and I hate to intentionally hurt people." I huffed. "It didn't even have to be all that, but it's like I can't communicate with him effectively without going to hell's level of low. And this is the second time he's tried to insult me."

"I don't think you'll have to worry about him ever again in life. I should've pulled out my phone and recorded it."

"EJ, you are so silly." I chuckled.

Her expression turned serious. "Choc, can I ask you something?"

"What?"

"Did you mean what you said?" Her lips twitched as she tried to maintain a serious face. "The bigger and better part, was there any truth to it?"

"Sweetie, not one lie was told!" We fell back on my bed howling in laughter.

***

"Where have you been?! I've been blowing your phone up!" April blurted when we finally touched bases.

"Out, living life." I sat the phone on the countertop as I reached up to grab my seasonings from the cabinet. "What's got you in a frenzy?"

"Have you seen Calvin? I think he's coming to Louisiana!"

"Girl," I scoffed. "He's come and gone. Oh, and I'm a slut."

"He called you a slut?!" April gasped. "Oh my God! I'm guessing he found out about Denim then."

"Girl, yes!" I cackled. Now that I wasn't in the moment, I found it to be sidesplitting. "Let me tell you what happened."

"Wow!" she gasped after getting the tea. "His feelings were just hurt. He may not have meant it."

"I don't care whether he did or didn't." I sliced through our new year cabbage and dropped it into the water. "And this isn't the first time he's tried to berate me."

"I'm sorry, Choc," she apologized. "I didn't know he was like that."

"Me either until two weeks ago. After speaking with his mother, I understand that a lot of Calvin's ways stem from his upbringing. He's never seen a properly balanced relationship. It's like he's just catching on. But he can't be mad at me for not wanting it anymore."

"Maybe this will be a lesson for him."

"Hopefully, it's a lesson for you too," I stated.

"What do you mean?"

"I hope you learned that you don't need to try to play matchmaker ever again in life!"

"Girl!" she hollered.

"I'm just kidding," I tittered. "But at least that chapter is officially closed. On to the next one!"

***

The music could be heard before we made it to Denim's door.

"They lit over here!" EJ grinned.

Mama shot her a look. "Good for them! But you better act like you have some sense when we get over here!"

"Leave her alone, Roz," Andrew interjected. "You need to go home if you gon' be uptight."

"Drew, you need to-" He cut her off with a kiss.

Laughing and shaking my head at their interaction, I rang the doorbell.

"Hey there, girl!" Ms. Dana opened the door and nearly squeezed the life out of me. "EJ! Rozzy!"

"Dana Dane!" Mama greeted her.

She eyed Andrew. "Girl, is this fine man yours?"

"Yes. This is Andrew." Mama beamed. "Andrew, this Dana, a crazy old friend."

"Nice to meet you." He smiled politely.

"Nice to meet you too. Now come on in and party with us." She stepped aside to let us cross the threshold. "We got food and drinks set up in the kitchen. Help yourself."

"Yes ma'am," I responded as I watched a middle aged man cut a rug in the middle of the living room.

I continue to survey the room, seeing a few people that I knew and a lot that I didn't. Denim was nowhere to be found.

"Ms. Dana, where's Denim?" I asked.

"Probably in his room. He's mad because he didn't know this many people were coming, but shit, neither did I." She shrugged.

Shaking my head, I went to find him.

I knocked lightly on the door before entering. "Sourpuss, you gotta come out of here and party with me!"

"Hey, Chocolate!" His eyes lit up for a second. "This shit is a mess."

"It ain't that bad. You're just not used to having these people in your house." I had a seat beside him. "I got something for you."

"A kiss I hope."

"You can get that too, but here." I held out my book of poems.

"I can't wait to dive into this." He grinned, opening it.

"Denny, no! Don't read it yet! At least not around me!"

"Ok." He laughed. "I won't."

He put it in the drawer of his nightstand. "But gimme a kiss."

Puckering my lips, I leaned towards him.

"Denman, you mama said we need more ice!" A little boy, who looked to be about three, burst into the room.

"Aww, shit!" he groaned. "You wanna ride with me?"

"Yes!" The little boy grinned.

"I wasn't talking to you, Mahzi, but you can come too." He grabbed his keys off the dresser.

***

"My mama is mad because my daddy is drunk," Mahzi chattered in the backseat.

"Alright, it's time for you to be quiet!" Denim chuckled.

"Leave him alone!" I laughed, wondering who his parents were.

"I hope our future kids don't be telling our business like that."

"They will."

"Can we get McDonald's?" Mahzi asked as Denim went to get the bags of ice.

"They're closed, baby," I replied.

He stood up in the backseat, looking across the street. "Can we get firecrackers?"

"You want some sparklers?"

"Naw, a rocket!"

"A rocket?!" I gasped before reaching behind me to tickle him.

"Yesss!" he screamed. "Can I get one?"

"You'll have to ask him." I pointed as Denim slid back into his seat.

"Ask me what?"

"She said I can get a rocket!" he blurted.

"You told him that?" Denim's eyes darted from me to the baby.

"I didn't say that! That little boy is a mess! I told him to ask you."

Denim gave him a stern look. "We already got rockets at home, but if you keep telling stories, I'm not gonna let you pop them."

"Alright. I'm sorry, Denman." He gave us puppy dog eyes that I couldn't resist.

"It's ok, baby."

"Mannn..." Denim smacked his lips and laughed. "Mahzi done found him a sucka."

Denim checked his watch as we exited the car and prepared to go into the house. "It's almost eleven. At twelve, we gon' shoot fireworks, and they gon' take their asses home."

"Denny, quit being a grouch!" I fussed. "We're gonna go in here, have a drink, and have a good time. And you're gonna dance with me."

"That's right, sis!" EJ laughed behind us. "Get his ass in check!"

I turned around to see her dragging Chris, who held a bottle of Casamigos.

"Hey, Chris!" I waved.

"What up, EJ and Chris!" Denim spoke.

"What's up?" Chris grinned.

EJ smiled at Mahzi. "Whose child have y'all kidnapped?"

"My stepsister's," Denim replied. "This is Mahzi."

She pinched his cheek. "Hey, Mahzi!"

"Is that juice?" Mazhi pointed at the bottle in Chris' hand.

"No, baby." I grabbed his hand. "Let's go inside."

***

We made our way into the kitchen with Mazhi right behind us. After grabbing some finger sandwiches, wings, cups of Hpnotiq, and juice for Mahzi, we sat at the island watching everybody else.

"Look at Roz!" I laughed at mama throwing it back on poor Andrew. "She was talking about EJ, but she's drunk."

"Shid, Ms. Roz is turnt! But look at my mama!" Denim hooted. "That lady doesn't have a lick of rhythm!"

My eyes searched the room for EJ. She stood in a corner with her phone out recording mama.

I nudged him and gestured in her direction. "Look at messy boots! She is never gonna let mama live this down."

Turning to Mahzi, I held a sandwich for him to bite.

"Is he over here bothering ya'll?" I gazed up and locked eyes with a tall shapely brown skinned woman.

"Naw. He good," Denim responded. "Mickey, this is Choc. Choc, this is my stepsister."

She grinned and extended a hand. "The girl you wouldn't shut up about on Christmas. Nice to meet you."

"Nice to meet you too." I grinned.

"I gotta introduce you to the rest of my people." Denim caught EJ's attention and beckoned her over. "This is my little sister, EJ and her boyfriend, Chris. Well, Choc's sister. Y'all, this is my stepsister, Mickey."

"Nice to meet you." She shook both of their hands. "Both of y'all are pretty. That must be y'all's mama." She pointed at mama.

"Yep. That's her," EJ stated.

"It was nice meeting you all. I'm gonna take my lil crumbsnatcher so you can enjoy your night in peace. Come on, Mahzi!" She tossed him on her hip. "Tell 'em bye!"

Beyonce's "Cuff It" began to play.

"This is my jam! Come on, Denny!" I hopped off the stool, pulling him along.

I feel like fallin' in love

I'm in the mood to fuck something up

EJ and I sang along at the top of our lungs and danced with our men and each other.

When that song ended, Juvenile's "Back That Ass Up" really got the party jumping.

"Uh-uh, Chocolate! We not even bout to play these games!" Denim hollered in my ear before leaving me to dance by myself.

***

"Alright, everybody! It's a little less than ten minutes until midnight! I need y'all to grab your cups and follow Denim!" Ms. Dana announced.

I grasped Denim's hand as he led us out of his back door and into the direction of the field.

Tonight it was illuminated with solar lights, and they'd set out a bunch of chairs for everyone to sit if we wanted. I found a seat on the opposite side of Mama, Andrew, EJ, and Chris while Denim went to help set up the fireworks.

My eyes roamed the vicinity from everyone sitting around to Denim, and lastly they landed on my family who were in the corner laughing amongst themselves. Realization hit me like a mack truck, and I couldn't control my tears.

Grief can be so painful, and the healing journey can be a rough one. As I sat there observing the people that I loved the most, I realized that I'd made it to an important point in mine.

It was a tragic event that broke me, not necessarily this place that I'd been avoiding. The sudden homesickness I'd experienced in California now made sense too. My spirit had been trying to tell me that it was time to come back. This was home, where I belonged.

I quickly swiped at my tears as Denim occupied the chair beside me. "I thought you were lighting firecrackers."

"No, indeed. I gotta earn a living. They not bout to blow my hand off." He reached underneath the chair for the beer he'd stashed. Finally, he gave me his full attention. "You crying?"

"Yes, Denny, I am. I'm in my feelings, but I'm not sad."

With the pads of his thumbs, he wiped the other tears that cascaded. "You understand what I was saying earlier, huh?"

"Mhmm." I nodded.

"Alright, y'all! Time to count it down!" Ms. Dana announced. "Ten..."

"Nine... eight... seven... six... five... four... three... two... one," Denim and I chanted. "Happy New Ye-!"

Before I could get all of the words out, his lips locked with mine as the fireworks shrilled and illuminated the sky.

The End

Connect With Me

Facebook page: DeAndrea Hughes

Facebook group: It's A De Thang

Instagram: de_wroteit

Catalog

The Winter Sisters 1 & 2

Into The Arms of A Real One

Too Good To Let Go: Star & Marco

Made in the USA
Monee, IL
07 January 2023